With a scream of feminine fury, Itzel ran straight for Dr. Tracy, having identified him as the man ultimately responsible for Hector's death. She attacked him with her fingernails, raking them across his face. Spittle flew from between her clenched lips and her eyes were wild… it felt good to hurt him but the moment was over far too soon. Tracy backhanded her hard enough to rattle her teeth and split her upper lip. She toppled over, landing hard on her left hip.

The adrenaline that had propelled her into battle was suddenly gone, having left her as quickly as it had appeared. Her shoulders shook and she thought of her parents… would they ever know what had happened to her? Would they think she and Hector had run off together? Her mother would be heartbroken.

She looked up into Tracy's face but what she saw defied her expectations. Where she'd scratched his cheek, there was a gaping wound. Flesh hung by a tiny scrap to his face but it was what lay beneath that confused her. First, there was no blood… and second, there appeared to be a second layer of skin that had now been exposed.

And it was *blue*.

"Who are you?" Itzel whispered but she knew that a better question would have been, '*What* are you?'

The man reached up and peeled away the flap of skin, tossing it aside. He smiled cruelly and said, "I'm Evil, my dear."

Captain Action™—Cry of the Jungle Lord
Story © 2017 Barry Reese and Jim Beard

The character "Captain Action" is © & ™ CA Enterprises LLC 2017.
All Rights Reserved.

Published by Airship 27 Productions
www.airship27.com
www.airship27hangar.com

Interior illustrations © 2017 Rob Davis
Cover illustration © 2017 Ted Hammond

Editor: Ron Fortier
Associate Editor: Gordon Dymowski
Production and design by Rob Davis
Marketiing and Promotions Manager: Michael Vance

ISBN-10: 1-946183-23-7
ISBN-13: 978-1-946183-23-1

Printed in the United States of America

10 9 8 7 6 5 4 3 2 1

CRY OF THE JUNGLE LORD

BY BARRY REESE AND JIM BEARD

AIRSHIP 27 PRODUCTIONS

PROLOGUE

Late 1968

Itzel crouched in the darkness, a smile touching her cupid-bow lips. Her brown hair fell straight over her shoulders and her almond-colored eyes seemed to glitter in the moonlight. She wore a knee-length gypsy-style skirt and a peasant blouse, with sandals under her feet. The clothes had been purchased during her last visit to the closest major city and had cost every peso she owned but they were worth it.

"It's so beautiful," she whispered, looking around at the area. She and her boyfriend had come out here to the middle of nowhere because she wanted to see the so-called Sky Rock that had supposedly fallen from the heavens years before. The rock itself wasn't much to look at but the scenery was breathtaking.

"*You're* beautiful," a male voice whispered from the shadows that surrounded her.

Her smile turned into a mischievous smirk. Hector had agreed to bring her here because he wanted to be alone with her. He'd impatiently played her little game for almost three months now, gradually being allowed more and more liberties. Tonight he hoped to see her naked but Itzel wasn't certain she'd go that far.

She couldn't see him, of course. He was too good at blending into the night, dressed as he was in dark clothing. But she could sense him watching her, his eyes roving over her form. She felt both thrilled and annoyed at how hungry he was for her body.

Trying to take her mind off the sexual tension, she went over all the things she had learned about the jungles of the Yucatan in school and from her own private studies.

The areas between northern Guatemala, Mexico and western Belize were home to the largest continuous tracts of tropical rainforests in Central America. Since the Yucatan Peninsula comprised a significant proportion of the ancient Maya Lowlands, the jungles housed numerous archaeological sites, with some of the most famous being Tulum, Uxmal and Chichen Itza. Many people boasted of Mayan ancestry and the Mayan languages were still widely spoken. Itzel's own name was Mayan in origin, meaning "moon goddess" or "she of the rainbow."

Hector emerged from the shadows, his hands slipping around Itzel's

5

waist from behind. He pulled her hard against him and she sighed before laughing softly. "Are you thinking what I'm thinking?" he asked.

"I was trying to remember everything that Prof. Gutierrez told us in class."

"Okay, that's not at all what I was hoping you'd say…"

Itzel pulled away, a blush on her cheeks. "We can kiss if you want."

Hector's disappointment was so evident that Itzel laughed at him. When he turned away angrily, she felt a sudden burst of guilt and quickly grabbed him by the hand.

"I'm sorry, Hector. I don't mean to tease you."

"Then let me…you know…"

An odd noise suddenly disturbed them and Hector pulled her close. "That's a car engine. Someone's coming."

Instinctively sensing that they shouldn't be seen, the duo retreated into the trees, their bodies pressed tightly against one another as they watched the scene.

As if on cue, the sounds of a truck driving up the dirt road split the night. It was a pickup truck, with two men seated in the front and three more riding in the bed. The trio in the back of the truck wore rifles slung over the shoulders. They were swarthy-skinned and dressed in threadbare shirts and dirty trousers.

The man behind the wheel was much more refined. He brought the truck to a stop just in front one of the larger ruins. He opened the door and stepped out, looking wildly out of place in his Nehru jacket, sandals and a large golden amulet that hung low on his chest. His longish blond hair fell straight down his back and he sported a mustache and forked beard.

From the passenger side emerged a nervous-looking Mexican, dressed in an ill-fitting shirt that was stretched tightly across an ample midsection. "This is it, Señor! The Sky Rock!"

The long-haired man frowned and moved past the Mexican. "I thought you said that the area was remote, Pepe."

"Uh…it is, Dr. Tracy! You saw how long it took us to get here!"

Rubbing his hands across the Nehru jacket, Tracy said, "Then why is there another vehicle parked here?"

Pepe looked around in the gloom, his eyes finally settling on the jeep that belonged to Hector's father. "Madre de dios," he whispered.

Dr. Tracy gestured to the armed men he'd arrive with. "Look around."

■ ■ ■

"Who are they?" Itzel asked fearfully.

"I don't know…but they look like trouble." Hector grabbed her by the hand and yanked her further into the jungle. "We need to get out of here."

Itzel stood firm. "It's too late."

"What do you mean—?" Hector froze when he turned to see that one of the armed men had already spotted them. The man had a rifle pointed directly at them and he shouted for them to stay where they were.

Hector stepped in front of Itzel, protecting her from the gunman. The gallant action occurred so naturally that it impressed Itzel greatly. She suddenly felt sorry that she'd never gone all the way with him.

The gunman gestured with the barrel of the gun. "Come out into the clearing."

Hector and Itzel emerged, coming face-to-face with the man called Dr. Tracy. Up close, Itzel couldn't help but think that he looked like an odd mix of college professor, hippie and cult leader.

"We don't want any trouble," Hector said.

Dr. Tracy smiled. "Neither do we."

"So…we can go? I promise we won't tell anyone that we saw you." Hector tried to look as friendly as possible, smiling so broadly that he looked almost cartoonish.

The smile faded a bit on Tracy's features. "I appreciate that. I really do…Unfortunately, my business here is so important that I can't take that chance." He gave a shrug of his shoulders. "Dreadfully sorry."

Hector blinked in confusion but realization dawned quickly as the gunman that had led them into the clearing suddenly opened fire. Two bullets tore through the young man's skull, sending a splatter of gore all over Itzel. Her boyfriend's corpse hit the ground a second later.

The young woman stood there in shock for a moment and Dr. Tracy held up a hand to indicate that his man should wait before firing. Tracy watched with interest as a range of emotions played across the woman's face: shock, horror, concern and rage.

It was that last one that intrigued Tracy. Most people in his experience, especially the fairer sex, tended to fold under strain. Yet here was a slip of a girl that was obviously made of sterner stuff. He wanted to see how bold she truly was.

Itzel was no longer thinking rationally—if she had been, she would have known how helpless her situation really was. She might have pled for mercy or even run into the jungle…but what she did instead was doomed to failure.

With a scream of feminine fury, Itzel ran straight for Dr. Tracy, having identified him as the man ultimately responsible for Hector's death. She attacked him with her fingernails, raking them across his face. Spittle flew from between her clenched lips and her eyes were wild…it felt good to hurt him but the moment was over far too soon. Tracy backhanded her hard enough to rattle her teeth and split her upper lip. She toppled over, landing hard on her left hip.

The adrenaline that had propelled her into battle was suddenly gone, having left her as quickly as it had appeared. Her shoulders shook and she thought of her parents…would they ever know what had happened to her? Would they think she and Hector had run off together? Her mother would be heartbroken.

She looked up into Tracy's face but what she saw defied her expectations. Where she'd scratched his cheek, there was a gaping wound. Flesh hung by a tiny scrap to his face but it was what lay beneath that confused her. First, there was no blood…and second, there appeared to be a second layer of skin that had now been exposed.

And it was *blue*.

"Who are you?" Itzel whispered but she knew that a better question would have been, '*What* are you?'

The man reached up and peeled away the flap of skin, tossing it aside. He smiled cruelly and said, "I'm Evil, my dear."

ONE: JUNGLE ACTION

1969

Miles Benson Drake swung his machete, chopping his way through the thick undergrowth. It was slow going and not for the first time he wondered if his guide thought he was being paid by the hour. They certainly seemed to be taking a circuitous route through the jungle. Under other circumstances, the trip might have been a lovely one but he had little patience for sightseeing at the moment.

Stopping under a gorgeous example of Blue Jacaranda, Drake exhaled, making a show of being more tired than he was. The Blue Jacaranda was over fifty feet tall and covered with gigantic, lilac-covered bouquets. The scent was enticing and very feminine. It made him think of someone in particular but the memory was not one that he wanted to dwell upon.

"How much further?" he asked, wiping sweat from his brow.

His guide, a heavyset man with deeply bronzed skin, shook his head before answering. Pablo wasn't the cheapest guide out there but he had the reputation for being one of the best. He wore a threadbare shirt that was transparent with sweat and khaki shorts. Atop his head was a broad-brimmed hat that he now removed to fan himself. The heat was oppressive. "Hard to say," Pablo answered in heavily accented English. "My sources tell me that the place lies near Sky Rock but I don't know in what direction or how close "near" means to them."

Drake looked around, his eyes narrowing. He had come here investigating reports of someone building something large in the Yucatan Peninsula…something that required large purchases of building materials and a lot of cheap labor. Chatter in the intelligence circles seemed to connect the mysterious construction project with the looming launch of the first manned mission to the moon, which was even now being prepared across the gulf in Florida. Given the importance of that mission, Drake had been dispatched to make sure there was no potential threat at play.

It was a long-shot but Drake had jumped at the mission opportunity. He craved action the way most men desired rest and relaxation. Indeed, that inability to stay out of harm's way had led him to be dubbed 'Captain Action' by the public and he'd become the de facto public face of the A.C.T.I.O.N. Directorate. A.C.T.I.O.N. was an acronym for "Advanced Command for Telluric Interdiction Observation and Nullification" and they were ostensibly Earth's primary defense against alien incursion. Just as often, however, Captain Action and cohorts ended up battling against threats of a terrestrial origin.

Pablo had no idea that he was in the company of the famous hero, however. Drake was in disguise, utilizing one of his many false identities—indeed, his very appearance was unrecognizable as that of Miles Drake. Plastiderm, an amazing clay-like substance that the Directorate had formulated from captured alien technology, allowed Drake to reshape his features into almost any shape imaginable. Coupled with his uncanny acting abilities, Drake could vanish into another identity with ease. As Jack Remick, he'd hired Pablo under the guise of being a mercenary seeking to find a hidden base in the jungle, where he hoped to secure work.

Remick was supposed to be slightly older than Drake, with graying temples and a dimpled chin. His eyes were also a different color and he had the slightest paunch, as if he were a fit man just beginning to slide into middle age. He wore shorts and a safari-style shirt with a backpack slung over his shoulders. Within that backpack was the uniform and weaponry familiar to the world as belonging to Captain Action.

"Señor?"

Drake had spotted something up ahead, his keen eyes detecting something that even Pablo had missed. He surged ahead, hacking with renewed vigor and forcing his guide to hurry along in an attempt to keep up.

They suddenly entered a small clearing, spotting a makeshift road a hundred yards or so away. It had obviously been used frequently and recently—the ground showed clear signs of heavy vehicles having moved across it in a regular pattern. "Bingo," he whispered. In a louder voice, he said, "We're on to something, Pablo."

"*Si*—and there's Sky Rock." The native guide was pointing at a large rock that jutted out of the ground. It wasn't native to this area and Drake recognized that it was a large chunk of meteorite—given how deeply it was embedded into the earth; it must have fallen hundreds if not thousands of years ago. Locals had probably long forgotten the details but they obviously remembered that it had come from the sky, hence the name. He vaguely recalled hearing that such rocks weren't uncommon in the area and he wondered how many more he might stumble across before his adventure was over.

He pushed on past the meteor, following the path until it suddenly veered off to the west. The road from that point forward was more start and stop, without any one definite path chosen. The Captain could see signs that the original road had once continued on in a straight direction but that area was no longer fresh, indicating that it had been abandoned for some reason.

It was almost as if whoever had been using this road had suddenly decided that it was no longer safe or worthwhile to maintain it—and they had since tried other routes without any real consensus.

Kneeling down, Drake examined the soil. He dug through some of it with his fingers, examining it closely. It was moist to the touch, even down farther than the humidity should have affected. "Are there any underground streams around here?" he asked.

"Si," Pablo answered. "The entire area is filled with them—and there are cave systems under us, as well."

Drake frowned. Groundwater had the potential to dissolve the carbonate cement that held sandstone particles together. The particles were then swept away by the water, gradually forming a void. The process was known as suffosion but few people outside of scientific circles knew that name for it. The results of suffosion, however, were known by almost everyone: sinkholes.

A sudden scream from Pablo made Drake snap to his feet. He turned to see that the guide was no longer standing off to the side—instead, his hands and the top of his head were all that were visible. The ground beneath Pablo's feet had given way and only quick thinking—or luck— had saved the man's life. He wouldn't survive much longer without help, however, as his fingers were starting to slip.

"Hang on!" Captain Action yelled. Any attempt at hiding his natural athleticism was tossed aside now that someone's life was at stake. Tossing aside his machete, he sprinted towards the sinkhole, leaping quickly from one foot to the other in an attempt to avoid the ever-widening gap. He dropped down beside Pablo, who stared at him with wide eyes. The two men hung side-by-side, their fingers dipping deep into the soft earth. At any moment, the ground they were holding onto could slip away, plunging them to their doom. A quick glance below showed that the fall was more than enough to kill a man, even with a stream flowing down below.

"What are you doing, señor? You're going to die with me!"

"Thanks for the faith, Pablo," he muttered. He inched closer and wrapped one hand around Pablo's waist. His grip was difficult due to the sweat on the other man's body but he held firm. "I'm going to lift you up but you've got to help me—use your feet as best you can to shove your body out of the hole. On three—understand?"

Pablo nodded, his face contorted by fear. The guide wasn't exactly what Miles would call an exemplar of bravery but he was certainly made of sterner stuff than most. Even now, with death seemingly at hand, Pablo wasn't hysterical. Scared, certainly, but far from incapable of following orders.

Drake counted out loud and on cue, he lifted the heavyset man up. Pablo's shoes scrabbled to get purchase but just when Drake felt his shoulders starting to give out, the guide was up and out, crawling away to safety.

Captain Action took a second to compose himself, readjusting his grip. For a moment he had held both his and Pablo's weight with just one hand. He tensed and then raised himself above the rim of the sinkhole. What he saw waiting for him was almost shocking enough to cause him to drop back down—Pablo was on his back, too frightened to make any sound. Pacing back and forth in front of him was a jaguar, one that had been attracted by Pablo's scream.

Drake clambered out of the hole and shrugged off his backpack, quickly opening it as the jaguar suddenly took notice of him. The big cat growled low in its throat and looked from Pablo to Drake, obviously trying to decide which one merited the most attention. The big cat was the third-largest feline in the world, trailing behind only the tiger and the lion—but it was by far the largest in the Americas. When they were properly motivated by hunger or a desire to protect their young, they could be fierce foes—and Drake sensed that the one before him was in dire need of sustenance. It wasn't going to be easily scared away.

He pulled from the backpack a most unusual weapon—a short sword with a jagged lightning-bolt edge. Captain Action had found the cutlass in a cache of alien technology years before and A.C.T.I.O.N. had pieced together some of its fascinating history. The weapon had popped up here and there throughout history and some of the big brains back at headquarters even thought it might be the archetype that similar swords from the ancient Greek machaira to the more recent variety of naval cutlasses were drawn from.

The full range of the sword's powers was still unknown but it was forged of orichalcun, a mysterious metal that had proven to be virtually unbreakable. It also possessed the ability to attract and absorb electrical energy, providing a powerful defense to its wielder.

Drake knew that he only needed the cutlass to function in its most basic of uses now—the jaguar was a purely physical foe, after all.

Captain Action moved towards the big cat and the two combatants circled each other while Pablo watched in stunned silence.

The jaguar struck first, leaping forward and taking a wipe with its razor sharp claws. Drake avoided the worst of it but the jaguar still struck him in the upper thigh area of his left leg, slashing his pants and drawing blood.

With a roar of his own, Captain Action retaliated. His cutlass whistled through the air, the flat part of the blade striking the jaguar on the side of its skull. Given the choice, the Captain wanted to avoid killing the beast—it wasn't evil, being driven to this assault only by its own need for sustenance.

The jaguar refused to be driven away after the harsh blow, however. It shook its head from side to side and growled again before leaping towards the human.

Cursing under his breath, Captain Action spun about and slammed the flat of the blade down atop the beast's back. It reacted with a loud yelp of pain but still continued on—it pounced towards him and swept its claws towards his legs once more but this time the Captain was prepared. He timed it so he danced away from the beast, avoiding its claws and teeth.

The jaguar roared in impotent fury. It tensed and crouched before leaping into the air, aiming for the hero's head. It would have been all too easy for Captain Action to stab upward with his sword, disemboweling the big cat. He refused to kill it so he simply allowed it to pass overhead and then he whirled about to throw himself onto its back. He tossed down his sword and wrapped his arms around its throat, applying pressure. He held on for dear life as the great feline thrashed about in an attempt to toss him off…but eventually the creature succumbed to the lack of oxygen. It slipped to the earth and its eyes grew heavy…then closed.

Panting, the Captain slid off the big cat's unconscious form. He knelt quickly to pluck up his sword and was headed to do the same to the backpack when he realized that Pablo was not alone. The guide was on his feet now, looking at Drake with open awe…but it was the woman that was standing alongside him that made the hero's breast seize up with emotion.

When he'd first met her, she'd been in disguise as a Russian defector… an expert in radiation that helped play a key part in an adventure that spanned several continents. She'd eventually been revealed to be an exiled member of a subterranean culture, located deep beneath Siberia. He'd fallen in love with her and felt that she harbored many of the same feelings for him. Unfortunately, she'd apparently died and he'd fallen into a deep funk that had only ended when she'd reappeared during one of Drake's follow-up missions in Japan. On both occasions, the madman known as Dr. Evil had been present but in the end, Drake had liberated his beloved from the madman's clutches. She'd returned home to New Lake, leaving Drake once again with an aching heart.

But here she was, looking beautiful as ever. Golden hair that fell past her shoulders and full lips that were curved upward at the ends in a smile. She wore jodhpurs and a white safari shirt that strained to hold her womanly curves.

Uliana Ulanova took a step towards him and without a word, they embraced.

TWO: REUNIONS

I knew it was you, even through your disguise—and as soon as I saw your sword, I knew it couldn't be anyone else."

Drake pulled back, staring into the eyes of the woman he loved. Her familiar and unique scent filled his nostrils, making his head swim. "Uliana…what are you doing here?"

Before she could answer, another familiar voice spoke up.

"She is with me, comrade."

Captain Action glanced to his right, where a slender figure had emerged from the jungle. He wore clothing that looked a lot like his old Russian military garb, though it was now sans insignia of any kind. His skin was startlingly pale and his eyes unnaturally pink. The albino was known as Juthrbog and he'd been a part of the same strange case that had led Drake to the underground city of New Lake. "Why is *he* here?" Drake asked through clenched teeth.

The warmth in Uliana's expression seemed to shift and she moved towards Juthrbog, saying, "He's my partner, Miles. He's helping me track down Dr. Evil."

Drake flinched as if struck. Surely he hadn't stumbled onto another of that madman's plans...? What unseen force bound him to Evil? Why did they seem destined to continually end up trapped in each other's orbit? "You think Evil's here in the Yucatan?"

It was Juthrbog that replied. His voice was silvery smooth, almost devoid of emotion. With his ramrod-straight posture and hands clasped behind his back, he seemed almost robotic. "Our sources indicate that he arrived in the Yucatan several months ago. There has been a large influx of money in the area and rumors of fortifications being built in the jungle."

"I'm here for the same reason," Drake said. "Though I didn't know about any possible connection to Dr. Evil." Turning his gaze back to Uliana, he asked, "How are things in New Lake?"

"Difficult," she said evasively. He knew her well enough to know that she didn't want to discuss it further.

"We should combine efforts," Drake said, a trifle too quickly.

"Inadvisable," Juthrbog warned.

"And why is that?" Drake asked. Though he thought Juthrbog wanted to atone for some of the mistakes he'd made in the past, he found it hard to trust the albino. Plus, there was the way that Juthrbog looked at Uliana... for someone that was generally so emotionless, it seemed an awful lot like protectiveness. "Do you have something to hide, Juthrbog?"

"Miles!" Uliana blurted out. "What's wrong with you? Juthrbog has proven his loyalty to me." She crossed her arms over her chest. "I think he's right. We're here for our own purposes and if we get involved with you, you're going to want to keep A.C.T.I.O.N. appraised of all our movements."

"So you're just going to leave? A quick hello and then you're gone?"

Uliana fixed him with her steely gaze and for a moment, he wondered if he really knew her at all. All their interactions had come in moments of high stress and he knew very well that such situations could create false impressions of intimacy. "Miles, I'm sure we'll see each other again...the Yucatan is only so large, after all."

Whirling about, she set off towards one of the three paths that led deeper into the jungle. Juthrbog remained where he was for a moment more, looking hard at Drake.

"You have something to say?" Captain Action asked.

"Only that if you truly care about her, you'll leave her to pursue her own destiny. A life with you would mean setting aside all of her goals and responsibilities...and she will never be satisfied as your housewife."

"I'd never ask her to be. She needs adventure...just like I do. We're two sides of the same coin."

Juthrbog lowered his voice. "Then why don't you turn your back on A.C.T.I.O.N. and join her in her quest to help New Lake?"

Drake hesitated...he'd had this conversation already, with Uliana herself. In the end, they'd parted, knowing that each had their own duties. He'd told himself that he could have left A.C.T.I.O.N. if she'd really pushed him to but he knew in his heart of hearts that he wouldn't have.

"That's what I thought, comrade. Be safe in your travels...and try to stay out of our way."

■ ■ ■

"Señor?"

Drake looked over at Pablo, who was staring at the jaguar. The big cat had begun to stir. "We need to get moving."

"I am going back to town."

"What? Why? I paid you to help me find the settlement out here."

"Si...but it will be dark soon and we've just barely survived two brushes with death. Plus, I realize that I am in over my head. The past few minutes...I have understood nothing! And I do not want to."

Drake had to smile at that. Sometimes he forgot how bizarre his life must seem to people on the outside. A part of him wanted to continue on, in hopes of finding the truth about what was going on before Uliana and Juthrbog did...but he also knew that he needed to report back in. If Dr. Evil was involved in all this, that made the mission all the more important. "Okay, Pablo...lead the way. I'll follow."

Pablo looked visibly pleased, having obviously expected Drake to put up a fight over his decision. He quickly started heading back and Drake cast only a brief glance in the direction that Uliana had gone before he followed suit.

THREE: La MaRSOPa

Pablo fled without saying goodbye as soon as they returned to the local town. Drake didn't really blame him but he wondered if he'd be able to convince the man to lead him back into the jungle. Probably not, he mused.

Returning to his hotel room, Drake reached up and peeled the plastiderm mask off his face. He tossed it into his bed and scratched his chin. He felt ill at ease and told himself that it was because Dr. Evil was supposedly nearby…but the truth was that little spat with Uliana troubled him.

Trying to avoid thinking about her, he retrieved the components of his transmitter device and quickly assembled them. Within seconds, he was connected to Major General Harlan James Weston, the acting head of the A.C.T.I.O.N. Directorate.

"Captain, I've been waiting to hear from you." The General's tone was gruff but Drake considered him one of his most trusted friends—even if neither would ever admit it.

"Sorry for keeping you waiting, General. I found some signs of activity in the jungle but nothing conclusive."

When Drake paused, the General picked up on it. "And—?"

"Uliana is here, with that strange Russian named Juthrbog."

The General sighed audibly. "I don't need this mission getting compromised by your feelings, Captain. We've been down this road before, remember?"

Drake didn't need the reminder. He'd nearly screwed a major mission in Japan when his concern for Uliana's well-being took precedence. "I won't let you down, Harl," he promised. "There's more—Uliana is here looking for Dr. Evil."

"Dammit all!" The General exclaimed. "That lunatic pops up again and again, doesn't he?"

"Maybe this will be the last time."

"You don't mean that, Miles. You want to see him stand trial for his crimes as much as I do, probably more, given your history with him."

Drake didn't answer right away. A part of him wanted to end Evil's threat permanently but he tried to avoid killing whenever possible. He heard footsteps in the hall and said, "I think someone's here, Harl. I better go."

"Not yet," the General commanded. "That's probably your local contact."

"What local contact…?"

"We made some overtures to the Mexican government and found out that our quarry may have been moved up the coast to the Northeast. Whatever you found today is either a few weeks old or just signs of them moving materials to their new location. In exchange for the information, they demanded the right to have their top agent join you on the mission."

"Harl, how could you?"

"You have your orders, Captain."

Frowning, Drake answered with a terse "Yes, sir."

A knock at the door caused the Captain to hurry up and disassemble the transmitter. He shoved it under his bed and walked towards the door.

It made sense why the Directorate wanted him to be on his best behavior. Relations between the U.S. and Mexico had begun to warm after some tense moments in the early part of the decade. The Mexican Government had praised Castro's Revolution and refused to cut ties with them, even after President Kennedy had pressured them to do so. On the other hand, Mexico appreciated that the United States had stayed out of their local politics—when student protests had threatened to destabilize the country prior to Mexico's hosting of the 1968 Olympics, America had watched in silence as the riots were put down with violence. If the two neighbors were going to stride arm-in-arm into the next decade, both sides needed to make overtures of peace.

With a frown on his face, Drake unlocked the door and flung it open. He wasn't sure who Mexico's "top agent" was but he pretty sure it wouldn't be anyone that he'd enjoy working with—professional rivalry existed in the intelligence community just as much, if not more, than everywhere else.

The person standing there was hardly what he'd expected, however.

It was a stunningly attractive woman that he pegged to be in her late twenties, with almond-colored skin and brown eyes. Her full lips were formed into an amused smile and from the laugh lines at the corner of her mouth he knew that she was someone that grinned often and easily. Her body was nicely proportioned, with the right amount of curves in all the correct places—and they were nicely showed off by her attire: olive-

"You have your orders, Captain."

colored shorts and a white tank top over which she wore an unbuttoned shirt of light green. There was a slight bulge under her over shirt on the right side of her hip and he recognized the shape as a handgun.

"Señor Drake?"

Captain Action smiled in greeting. "I'm going by the name Jack Remick, actually. And you are—?"

"Selena Rubio." She offered him a hand and he took it, noting that her skin was soft and inviting. "You're a bit of a legend, Señor. It's going to be an honor working with you."

Drake stepped back to allow her to enter. After shutting the door, he said, "I appreciate the sentiment, Selena, but I have to be honest: I'd prefer to work alone on this one."

"Because of your ongoing feud with Dr. Evil or because of your feelings for Uliana Ulanova?"

Drake blinked in surprise. "How in the world—?"

Selena sat down on Drake's bed and crossed her long legs. She looked at him mischievously. "I've been following you ever since you arrived in town. I was ready to lend a hand when your man fell into the sinkhole but you seemed to have it all under control."

"That's impossible. I would have known if I were being tracked for that long."

She shrugged and said, "You are good...but I am better."

Drake was beginning to think that he might not like Miss Rubio after all.

As if sensing his mood, she stood back up and held her hands up in surrender. "I am sorry. You are taking my teasing too personally. I respect you very much and I was hoping to impress you—that is all."

"You really followed me that long?"

"Yes."

"Then I *am* impressed." Drake moved to the window and looked out onto the busy street. "I just heard from the head of the Directorate—he says that it looks like the operations might have shifted to the northeast. Have your people given you any details?"

"There is a town to the northeast known as La Primavera. It is about three or four hours away by jeep. Recently, the government has issued an evacuation notice because the water supply has become tainted. There is a good chance that whomever it is that has been buying up so many supplies is responsible for tainting the water. I think we should go there." Selena stepped close enough that Drake could smell her perfume. It was intoxicating. "Why did A.C.T.I.O.N. send you here? All I have been told is that someone has been making large purchases and building in the jungle...but you must know more if they would bother sending the famous Captain Action to investigate! You came even before you knew about Dr. Evil!"

Captain Action suspected that she knew more than she was letting on—she probably just wanted to test him to see how truthful he intended to be with her. "Rumor has it that whatever is going on here is related to the moon launch. We can't let that happen...and if Dr. Evil is behind it all, then that's even more of a concern." He moved to the small closet and opened the folding door that hid his belon gings. His Captain Action togs were hanging there and he took them off their hangar. "I'm going to change into my 'work clothes'—I can wear them underneath a shirt and slacks. If we find any trouble at this La Primavera, I'd like to be able to greet it in style."

Selena nodded, turning away to give him privacy to change. She caught his reflection in the mirror, however, and saw his lean, well-muscled body come into view as he stripped out of the clothes he'd worn into the jungle. His torso was lined with scars from dozens of battles—she wondered what stories lay behind each one of them. With a slightly husky voice, she asked, "The hat you sometimes wear...where did you get it? It looks like something a seaman would wear."

"You're right about that...I found it on a mission and liked it. Not much more than that. Now it's tradition—heck, I've risked life and limb to get that silly hat back a time or two." He finished pulling on his Action attire and snapped his belt on. He then pulled on clothing over the skin-tight suit. The hat looked doubly silly when worn with street clothes but there was something undeniably attractive about it nonetheless.

When he turned around, Selena was looking directly at him; her eyes alight with some secret humor.

"So, 'Captain Action', do you want to get started on this team-up of ours?"

"No point in waiting, I suppose." He paused as he pulled his backpack on—as before, it contained his weapons and a few other bits of equipment. "Do you have a codename you'd like me to use when we're in the field?"

She smirked slightly and said, "Yes. My handlers refer to me as La Marsopa."

Drake ran through his knowledge of Spanish and blurted out, "The Porpoise?"

"If you're lucky, you might get to see how I earned that name."

The way she laughed made him very curious indeed.

■ ■ ■

Drake had to admit that La Marsopa was an impressive woman—she managed to secure a jeep with provisions in less than half the time he would have anticipated. When it came time for them to leave town, he automatically assumed that he'd be driving—but she beat him to the punch, sliding behind the wheel with a playful wink.

"I like to be in control, Señor Drake. You don't mind a woman taking the lead, do you?"

"I'm all in favor of equal rights," he murmured. He got into the passenger seat, putting his backpack between his knees.

"That's good…I know that men of your generation sometimes have trouble with that."

Drake's mouth fell open. "My generation…? How old do you think I am?"

"Maybe I shouldn't answer that," she said, pressing her foot down on the accelerator. The jeep surged forward and Drake was thrown back in his seat. She laughed gaily as they rocketed through the narrow streets, pedestrians scurrying to get out of their way.

"Where did you learn how to drive?" he asked as they reached the edge of town.

"Self-taught."

"I never would have guessed."

Selena slowed the car and Drake's attention was drawn to a man that stood in the center of their path. Unlike all the others, he refused to budge as she came closer—in fact, Drake tensed as she came so close to him before stopping that the jeep's bumper must have grazed the man's legs.

The fellow was tall and bronzed by exposure to the sun. He wore jungle camouflaged pants, shirt and hat. His beard was neatly trimmed and he peered out from under the brim of his hat with narrowed eyes that were a curiously gray color.

Captain Action was out of the vehicle in a flash, his electronic pistol in hand. The amazing weapon was capable of discharging 100,000 volts of electricity along a stream of ionized gas. Such an attack could stun an elephant and potentially kill a man. The downside was that the gun carried only three charges and made a loud racket as it charged up for each shot.

"Mind telling me why you're in our way?" the Captain asked.

The man looked from Selena to the Captain before he answered. "Well, I would have thought that was obvious: I'm here to save your lives."

FOUR: JACK

aptain Action stared into the stranger's gray eyes and wondered for a moment if the fellow was insane. "You'll have to give me a bit more than that to go on."

Selena was still seated in the driver's seat of the jeep, the engine idling. "He's nobody," she said with a tinge of annoyance in her voice. "Just push him aside and let's go."

Drake glanced back at her. "You know him?"

"She knows *of* me," the stranger said. "Quite a difference." He held out a callused hand and after a moment, Drake put away his gun and shook it. "Name's Jack, by the way. Jack Oat." Something in the way the man said his name gave Drake the distinct impression that he was making a joke of some kind.

"You can call me Captain Action."

Jack nodded as if he already knew that. "The hat gave it away."

"See?" Selena asked. "I told you it was weird to wear that thing." She revved the engine. "If you're going to talk to us, Jack, can you do it from the backseat? We're headed somewhere."

Jack gave a nod and strode towards the jeep, sliding into the backseat. Once Drake was settled back into the passenger side of the vehicle, Selena resumed her perilous driving into the jungle.

The Captain turned partially in his seat so he could look at Jack. "Let's hear it."

"I used to work for the Central Intelligence Agency. I was assigned to this region years ago—completed my mission but decided to stay for reasons of my own. Now I work with another group...one that focuses on getting things done, regardless of politics or the laws of modern man. We focus on justice, not the changing norms of society."

"Sounds a little shady," the Captain said.

"Depends on whether or not you're deserving of punishment," Jack retorted. "If you are, you're not going to be a fan of what we do. But if you're on the straight and narrow, you have nothing to fear from us."

Selena gave an un-ladylike snort of derision. "Jack here has been spotted at the scene of all kinds of trouble but nobody has ever been able to pin anything on him…and this is the first time I've ever heard that he's ex-CIA. Personally, I think he's just loco en la cabeza."

Drake narrowed his eyes and asked, "Why are you here? Don't tell me you've been tailing me, too?"

Jack blinked. "Has someone been following you?"

"Forget it—just explain yourself."

"My people have been looking into the strange situation at La Primavera and discovered that the Mexican government has been doing the same. I paid off a contact to tell me who was in charge of the investigation and they told me about the beauty behind the wheel. I didn't expect her to be with the famous Captain Action but life's full of surprises." Jack leaned forward, resting a hand on the back of the Captain's seat. "This is dangerous stuff—it's not just construction going on out in the jungle. People have been vanishing for awhile, too. Teenagers, mostly, but there's something going on out there and it's dangerous. Let me and my people handle it. You two can go back to the hotel, sip a few drinks and take the credit for our success. Don't get involved in this any further—I won't be able to protect you. There are things out in that jungle that you could never understand."

"Like what?"

Jack tapped Selena on the shoulder. "Stop the car."

She did so, pulling over to the side of the dirt road. "Now what?" she asked.

"This is where I get off." Jack stepped out of the jeep. He stood there with his hands on his hips. "Captain, I've heard many stories about you. This one mission won't change the legacy of heroism that you've built up. Just back off for once."

Drake shook his head. "You've got the wrong man, friend. If there's one thing I could never do, it's stand aside and let someone else do the dirty work for me. Now—are you going to answer my question or not?"

"Let's say that there are ghosts and phantoms in this area, Captain. Things that your fancy little gun won't be able to kill."

"I know what he's talking about," Selena said. "Just let him go and I'll fill you in on the details—not that it matters, since it's all a bunch of carp."

Both Drake and Jack looked at her in confusion.

"I think you mean crap," the Captain said. "Carp is a type of fish."

Selena shrugged. "Is his story like excrement or is it all fishy? Either way, it's nothing to get concerned about."

Jack grunted. "It's up to you, Captain. Take my advice or not...but I hope you'll prove smarter than your companion." Without another word, Jack turned and sprinted into the jungle. He vanished so quickly that he could have been an apparition, much like the ones he'd been talking about.

The Captain put a hand on Selena's leg and she jumped at the unexpected contact. "Don't start driving yet," he said.

"Move your hand, please," she replied. "You may be used to female agents throwing themselves at you but you're a little older than I like."

Drake did as she asked but he couldn't stop himself from frowning. The jabs about his age hit home a little more than he'd like to admit. "Is there anything else you know about this Jack character?"

"No," she admitted. "Like I said, he's been noticeable enough that we've tried to keep tabs on him but we've never been able to find out anything substantial."

"So you don't believe that he's part of some group?"

"If he is, the rest of them do better at hiding in the shadows than he does."

Drake considered that. Most people that thought of the Directorate pictured Captain Action first and foremost. He was the public face of the group and the one that posed for photographs when they were needed. As a result, most people had no idea of the full scope of the organization—that was partially by choice. Was Jack doing the same sort of thing?

The sound of a car approaching from the direction of the town they'd just left made Drake tense up. "Someone's coming," he hissed. He immediately began discarding his outer clothing, tossing it into the backseat. His colorful Captain Action attire came into view and he made sure that his cutlass was sheathed at his hip. "I have a hunch that whoever is coming isn't doing so by accident. Cut the engine."

Selena did so and the area was suddenly very quiet...until a van came zooming up alongside them. It skidded to a stop just past them on the road, the driver yanking the wheel so that they blocked the jeep's path. "Think they're about to ask for directions?" Selena asked. She pulled out her pistol, her lovely face suddenly drawn quite serious.

"I don't think so," the Captain replied. He spotted five men emerging from the van, each of them armed in some fashion. One of them held a rifle, two were carrying handguns and the other two had melee weapons—one wielded a baseball bat and the other brandished a nightstick, similar to the one used by police officers.

Selena and Captain Action stepped out of the jeep, each holding their guns at the ready. They had a sort of natural chemistry when it came to this and both fell into position a few feet away from each other—close enough to render aid but far enough apart do they wouldn't bump into one another if the violence turned personal.

The man with the baseball bat seemed to be the leader of the group—he pointed the weapon at Selena and spoke in Spanish. Drake was fluent in multiple languages though he'd learned that it was often advantageous to not let the locals be fully aware of that. "Señorita, you need to get back in the jeep. We know that your friend is an American—and Americans always have dinero. Let us talk to him alone and we'll let you go."

Selena's response was quick and to the point. "I'm going to shoot you in your kneecaps if you take one more step."

The men with guns responded by raising their weapons and training them on Selena and the Captain.

Drake couldn't resist. "I think this is the very definition of a Mexican standoff."

FIVE: VIOLENCE

Captain Action charged up his gun, the odd ratcheting noise sounding extremely loud in the still jungle air. The thieves exchanged concerned glances, worried about the unusual weapon that the American was holding. Their confusion wasn't enough to dissuade them from violence, however.

There were no birds singing and no insects buzzing…it was as if the world had stilled itself so that it could watch the proceedings without distraction.

The thug with the rifle fired first. His shot was intended for Captain Action but the hero was already in motion—he sprinted to his right and fell into a rolling motion. The bullet struck the ground a foot or two behind him.

There was bedlam now as Selena returned fire—her first shot was deadly accurate, hitting the man with the rifle in the throat. He fell back and lay twitching on the ground, his gurgling sounds audible even over the gunfire.

The two men with handguns shot at Selena but the Mexican woman was almost as fast as Captain Action himself. She ducked behind the jeep, flinching as one of the headlights shattered as a bullet struck it.

Captain Action took aim and fired his unique weapon. An ionized stream of electricity shot forth and caught the two gunmen in a single burst. They screamed as their bodies were buffeted by enough energy to stop a rhino.

Selena rose from her crouching position and took aim at the remaining men but they were smarter than their companions and had taken coverage behind their van. Without ranged weapons, they were pinned down and Captain Action motioned for Selena to cover him as he took the battle towards them.

Drake sprinted forward and came upon a man wielding a nightstick. The fellow struck quickly and Captain Action was unable to avoid the blow—it hit him hard in the left shoulder and sent a shock of pain all the way down to his fingertips.

The Mexican grinned excitedly, thinking that he was taking the lead in the battle—unfortunately for him, Drake was hardly down for the count. He struck the fellow with the barrel of his gun and knocked the man to his knees. He then jammed an elbow onto the back of the fellow's skull, rendering him unconscious. He'd managed to take him out without wasting one of the gun's charges, which pleased the Captain immensely—and he was also happy that he'd avoided killing anyone so far.

He heard a grunt of pain and whirled about—the man with the baseball bat had somehow managed to sneak around behind Selena and was swinging it like he was Willie McCovey. Selena barely avoided having her head bashed in and for a moment Captain Action worried that she was going to be killed—but then he saw that she had the situation under control. She struck back by driving a knee into the man's groin, causing him to topple forward in shock and pain. She then delivered a massive uppercut with the gun still in her hand—the blow sent one of the man's teeth flying out, accompanied by a stream of blood. She followed up by taking a few steps back and then unleashing a whirling leg kick that shattered the man's nose and knocked him onto his back.

As the man moaned in agony, Selena placed a foot on his chest and pointed her pistol at his face.

"Let him live, Selena."

The woman's beautiful face was twisted with rage, making her considerably less attractive. "We have ones you knocked out," she replied. "You don't understand how things work in Mexico. You have to send a strong message—if they come at you with a club, you have to hit them back with a gun. If they manage to hit you in the shoulder…you have to shoot them in the face."

Captain Action walked towards her, shaking his head. "He's down. It would be murder."

Selena glanced quickly at him, her eyes wide. "He's just a criminal. He was going to rob you of your money and then leave you for dead."

"He's a human being."

Her gaze flicked down to the electrical gun he was gripping with one hand. "Are you going to shoot me to save his life?"

"Are you going to make me?"

Selena grinned and relaxed, holstering her gun in the waistband of her shorts. "I'd heard stories about your mercy but I didn't quite believe them. How have you managed to stay alive this long with such a bleeding heart?"

Captain Action put away his pistol and ignored her question. He knelt beside the man that Selena had battered and yanked him up by his collar, bringing the thug's face close to his own. In Spanish, he asked, "Do you work for Jack? Did he slow us down so you and your men could catch up to us?"

The man mumbled something incoherent and the Captain realized that he was still too confused by pain to even understand the question.

"They're just thieves," Selena said. "There are many like them in these areas—they prey upon tourists and the weak." She turned her attention back to the jeep and examined it. There was superficial damage and they would be short one headlight but nothing that would delay their progress. "We've been delayed too long, Señor. I'd like to make it to La Primavera before nightfall."

Drake took the hint and stood up. He crossed back over to the jeep and asked, "What about these men? Are we just going to leave them out here?"

"You said you didn't want to kill them," Selena pointed out. Seeing his frown, she playfully rolled her eyes and pointed out the CB radio installed under the dashboard. "Use channel 22 and report the incident—a police patrol might come out and pick them up."

"Might?"

"This is not one of your American cities, Señor Drake. Things really are different here."

"Miles."

"Que?"

"Call me Miles. I get the feeling we're going to be together for awhile and you've already invited me to use your first name so…"

"Actually, you just did so without invitation. Very American—and male—of you."

"I can never tell when you're teasing me or being serious."

Selena laughed softly. "Sometimes I can't either. But…thank you, Miles. I appreciate the gesture."

The Captain reached for the radio and was about to pick up the handset when a peculiar sound echoed out of the jungle. It consisted of birdlike tweets interspersed with a series of woofs and howls. It lasted for nearly a full minute before it stopped—and while it sounded decidedly animalistic, there was a human quality to it that gave Drake pause. "What is that?"

Selena paused before answering. "Some people would say it's The Gibbon."

Drake caught her words and asked, "*The* Gibbon? What do you mean?"

"An old legend."

"I'd like to hear it."

Selena pursed her lips and nodded. "Fine. But I'll only tell you after you've made your radio call and we're on the road again. We're down to one headlight and I don't want to camp out in the jungle if I don't have to—so, we need to beat nightfall, remember?"

"You're a fierce taskmaster."

"It takes one to know one, *si*?"

SIX: GIBBON'S CRY

Selena drove like a madwoman but she had the quick reflexes of a professional racecar driver. Several times Captain Action was forced to grip his seat for dear life but no matter how narrow the path between trees or how close the wheels of the jeep came to a ledge, Selena never slowed down nor seemed to hesitate.

For the first time since they'd met, the Captain had an opportunity to study her at length. Her beauty was hard to ignore, of course, but upon closer inspection he could see a few signs here and there that told a story of adventure: a tiny scar behind her right ear, the telltale way she kept flicking her gaze from side to side and the way she kept her gun at such an angle that she could reach it easily.

"See anything you like?"

Drake smiled and looked away. "Sorry. Was I staring?"

"A bit—but it's okay. To be honest, I was beginning to wonder if you liked women. I usually warrant a little more flirting than you've been doing."

"I wasn't aware I'd done *any* flirting," he said.

"I was giving you the benefit of the doubt. I assumed you just weren't any good at it."

"You're not like any other agent I've ever met," Drake said. "Most of us are pretty grim. You seem like you actually enjoy all of this."

"I try to but it's not always easy. I've suffered losses along the way, just as I'm sure you have." She glanced quickly at him before turning her attention back to the road. "You wanted to know about El Gibon, *si*?"

Drake noticed that she was changing the subject from the topic of her 'losses' to something else but he let it go. If she decided to open up later on, he'd be more than glad to listen but they were on a job and he couldn't afford to lose sight of that. "I would. I assume that we're not dealing with a normal gibbon here—so is it some sort of man-beast like the Yeti?"

"Not quite. The locals say that hundreds of years ago a native hunter came upon a wounded gibbon of unusual size and color. Though the hunter had killed many such animals in his lifetime, he was touched by the humanity he saw in the gibbon's eyes. They experienced some sort of connection. The hunter stayed with the animal and tried to nurse it back to health but its injuries were too great. It died in his arms. Afterward, the hunter skinned the great beast and made a tunic out of its fur. Somehow this act transferred some of the animal's power onto him. He became more than a man; he was an extension to the animal kingdom…to the beating heart of the jungle. He returned to his people but to signify that he was no longer the man they knew, he took to wearing a mask. He was The Gibbon, sovereign protector of the jungle. No longer human, he is an immortal that hunts those that would prey upon the weak and defenseless. What you heard is supposedly his call—much like the gibbon with which he bonded, but full of humanity, as well."

Drake was silent for a moment, digesting all of that. He'd heard similar legends before but the fact that he himself had heard The Gibbon's call made him take this one just a bit more seriously.

"If we encounter any locals between here and La Primavera, you can ask them about it," Selena offered. "You won't get much in the way of a response, though."

"Why not?"

"Because the people love him. If an outsider comes asking about The Gibbon, they usually refuse to discuss it. The Gibbon will come to you if you're in need, not the other way around."

"I take it you're not a believer, given the way you've talked about it."

Selena gave another of those shrugs and Drake couldn't help but notice how the motion made her shoulders look inviting. He wasn't prone to falling for a woman too quickly but maybe his brief interaction with Uliana had emphasized the loneliness that he sometimes felt.

Either that or he was simply red-blooded enough to respond to the amazingly sexy woman sitting beside him.

"I've never seen The Gibbon," she admitted. "But I've heard his call. I suspect it's just some native having fun with tourists…or maybe it's an actual gibbon. Sometimes they can make very human-like sounds. But… no, I don't believe in The Gibbon story. For one thing, I've seen too many men and women die to believe that a man could become immortal by wearing a monkey skin."

Drake shook his head. "Honestly, I've seen stranger things."

"Like that Dr. Evil that you're always fighting?" Selena spotted a tightening of Drake's jaw and the clenching of his right hand into a fist. "I'm sorry for bringing him up…" she began but he cut her off with a wave of his left hand.

"No, it's all right. In fact, you probably need to know what you might be up against. Dr. Evil is a madman dedicated to nothing less than global domination. I believe in the justice system and always want to see it through but if there's one man out there that's deserving of an immediate judge, jury and executioner, he's probably the one."

Selena slowed as an animal darted across the road—a white-nosed coati cast a quick glance back at the vehicle before springing up into a tree. "So what's his story? I'm assuming he wasn't born with the name 'Evil.'"

"He used to be Dr. Stefan Tracy," Drake replied. "He was supposedly genetically modified by aliens, supposedly to unlock the ultimate potential of the human race. After his transformation he ended up running an

"Honestly, I've seen stranger things."

aerospace company as a front for his criminal activities but after one of our battles, he was outed to the public as a menace. Since then, he's embraced his role as a super-criminal. He killed his own daughter and son-in-law... and he would have done something unspeakable to his grandson had I not intervened. Sean—that's his grandson—lives with me now. I'm training him and he's got incredible potential."

Selena smiled. "You're an interesting man, Miles. Showing mercy to men that try to hurt you...adopting the grandson of your worst enemy..." She reached out and touched his arm lightly. "When all this is over, I'd love to get to know you better."

Drake blinked in surprise. She sounded casual but he couldn't help but wonder if she was implying something beyond simple friendship. Immediately he thought of Uliana—but was there really kind of future there? "I think I'd like that, Selena."

"Good—you know, I've always wanted to know about life during the First World War..."

Drake frowned. "I'm not that old...!"

Selena's laughter was so infectious that Drake found himself joining in before he knew it.

It felt good, he realized. It had been a long time since he'd chuckled so hard.

■ ■ ■

Twilight was beginning to settle over the jungle by the time they neared La Primavera. The town was little more than a village—Drake could see mostly one-story buildings and small pedestrian pathways, all located around a central well.

The road quickly became impassable as stragglers from the evacuation blocked their path. Drake attempted to converse with one or two of the locals as they streamed past the stopped jeep but no one seemed interested in talking. It was growing dark and these unfortunate few had missed most of the trucks that the government had sent. They had to reach their destinations on foot.

Pulling the jeep off the road, Selena stopped near some undergrowth. "I think the jeep will be okay here if you want to continue on into town."

Captain Action nodded. He reached up and adjusted his cap. "He's here," he said, more to himself than to Selena.

Still, his words made her look up quickly. "Dr. Evil?"

"No. Jack Oat."

Selena followed his gaze and frowned. Sure enough, the camouflage-wearing mystery man was in town. Three other men—all local, by the looks of them, were standing with him. Their attire matched his own; obviously designed to help them blend into the jungle.

Jack seemed to be observing the final evacuees but some sixth sense must have told him he was being watched because he abruptly looked directly at Selena and the Captain. He gave a brief wave and smiled enigmatically.

"Let's go talk to him," Drake said. "I have a feeling that there's a lot more to Mr. Oat than I first thought."

SEVEN: AMBUSH

Juthrbog stood at ramrod attention, one hand resting lightly on the hilt of the gun he wore holstered at his hip. As a member of the Russian military, he had developed a reputation for being a humorless but very effective soldier. His albino nature would have set him apart no matter what his personality had been like but he didn't mind the stares or whispers. They were the products of less evolved minds, ones that were so wound up in physical appearance that they couldn't accept him on a mental level.

Of course, he was not completely immune to physical appearances.

When he'd first laid eyes on Uliana Ulanova, he'd felt an unfamiliar set of sensations: his heart rate had sped up and a warmth had spread up to his cheeks, giving them a tiny bit more color than normal. She was more than beautiful; she was like some Nordic fantasy come to life—a physical manifestation of the myths of Freya, Hlin and Eostre.

And then he'd learned of her intelligence and grace…!

For the first time, he felt like he'd encountered someone that was more than his equal. She had stirred romantic feelings within him that he'd thought impossible. When the time had come for him to choose between his loyalty to the state and his growing affection for her, the choice had been a surprisingly simple one. He'd abandoned all of his responsibilities to follow her to a new life.

"Are you going to stand there on watch all night?"

Juthrbog turned towards Uliana, who was sitting on the ground beside a small campfire. The lengthening shadows had made it clear that day was beginning its slow transition into night and Uliana had opted to pause in their trek towards La Primavera. After leaving Captain Action, they had found people streaming away from the evacuated town and their stories had led Uliana to decide that was where they should go.

Juthrbog glanced at the three small lizards that were roasting on a spit over the fire. "There won't be much meat on those. You should have it."

"You need the protein as much as I do," she replied. "I also have the last of our provisions that we can use to stretch this into a full meal."

He looked around at the jungle once more and then moved to join her, sitting down on the opposite side of the fire. The lizards were beginning to smell quite good and he realized that he was actually quite hungry.

Uliana watched him closely, having learned to read his stony expressions. "Something's troubling you. Is it our mission?"

Juthrbog shifted his weight and gave a curt shake of his head. "No. It is nothing."

"Talk to me."

With a sigh, Juthrbog reached over to remove the spit from the fire. He examined the lizards and said, "I think they're ready." When he saw that she was still staring at him, he added, "I was not pleased to see Captain Action."

"Still holding grudges against him?"

"I…suppose that is so." The Russian handed one of the cooked lizards to Uliana and added, "I also have concerns that your feelings for the Captain might impede our mission."

Uliana paused just before taking a bite. "My…feelings…are always secondary to the betterment of my people. I have sworn to help revitalize them and Dr. Evil poses a continuing threat to their well-being."

"I have always admired your single-mindedness," Juthrbog responded. He tasted his own lizard and was pleasantly surprised by the flavor. While the traditional joke was that everything 'tasted like chicken,' lizard meat had a slightly different quality to it…a 'gamey' flavor that reminded him of the one time he had eaten wild venison. "Lizard meat is very popular in many Asian countries," he said as he continued to eat. "The Guandong province of China in particular considers it a delicacy—and in Vietnam, some types of lizards are believed to increase male virility."

Uliana smiled slightly and Juthrbog suddenly realized that he might have sounded suggestive in his turn of conversation. He was about to return to a safer line of discussion when Uliana suddenly tossed aside her lizard and stood up. He did the same, drawing his pistol. During their time together, he had learned to trust her instincts just as much as his own.

"We're in danger," she whispered.

Juthrbog saw her draw a large dagger from a scabbard strapped to her right thigh. They moved towards one another, naturally assuming a back-to-back stance to better protect their camp. "What did you hear?" he asked. He still hadn't picked up any unusual sounds.

"Nothing—that's the problem."

Juthrbog stared into the lengthening darkness and suddenly felt like a fool. The jungle, normally a cacophony of sound, was as silent as a tomb. He had been so distracted by his conversation with Uliana that he'd made a rookie mistake.

Suddenly the danger made itself manifest—a group of nearly a dozen armed men burst in from all sides, having surrounded the campsite. Their stealth was impressive and was a sure sign that these were no local thugs— these men were well-trained professionals. They wore combat fatigues, black full-face masks that revealed only their eyes and mouths and carried assault weapons.

Uliana showed no fear in the face of the overwhelming odds. While Juthrbog would have tried bargaining with the men, she said nothing before launching her attack.

She sprang forward like a jungle cat, moving with impressive speed and grace. Her blade sliced deep into the shoulder of the closest foe and his cry of pain was quickly joined by another's as she yanked her weapon free and spun about to drive it into the neck of a second man.

Juthrbog fired at a man whose rifle was raised in Uliana's direction. The bullet sent the fellow to the ground and the Russian was about to fire another when the men surrounding them opened fire. Their projectiles struck Juthrbog repeatedly and at least two caught Uliana as well—one in her upper shoulder and another in her buttocks.

Juthrbog looked down at a dart-like object that projected out of his neck…With some relief, he realized that neither he nor Uliana were about to die. For whatever reason, this group was planning to tranquilize them and take them captive.

He fell to his knees, the drugs quickly taking effect. He felt his gun slip from his hand as his eyes began to close. The last thing he saw was so impressive that he was smiling before his face hit the ground.

Uliana refused to surrender, even with the drugs from two tranquilizer darts coursing through her veins. She spun about, her blade catching the light from the rising moon. She plunged the knife into the chests of two different men and ducked under a blow from a third when he swung the butt of his rifle at her head. She stabbed him in the belly, a spray of red spattering her face.

She was up again in a flash, ready to continue the battle—but four more darts flew forth, striking her in her torso and leg. She staggered, futilely swiping at the air with her weapon. Unable to continue, she fell over, landing atop Juthrbog's unconscious body.

One of the remaining soldiers shook his head in amazement. The two targets had wreaked a lot more damage than anybody had expected. He pulled off his mask, revealing a handsome but cruel face. His red hair was shaved into a flattop. "Round 'em up," he said to the man at his side. "Make sure they're tied securely."

"What about our guys, Rex? Are we taking them back to get patched up?"

Rex pulled his lips into a sneer. "You know the rules—if they're strong enough to walk back under their own power, that's fine. But we don't coddle the weak."

EIGHT: MAN AND MYTH

Selena stood behind the bar, pouring herself a glass of bourbon. The tavern was very well stocked but the proprietor must have left in quite a hurry because the majority of his supply had been left behind. She looked over at Drake and Jack, who were seated together in the center of the bar. Jack's companions, decked out in their camouflage, seated nearby, keeping an eye on the front door.

One of the men had tried to strike up a conversation with Selena but she'd managed to dissuade him with a sharp stomp on his foot, followed by a promise to do worse the next time.

"Miles?" Selena asked. "Can I get you one?"

Drake looked at the bourbon and shook his head. Jack, however, grinned and winked. "I'll take one, if you don't mind."

Selena sauntered around the bar with her own drink in hand. "You can pour your own."

"You wound me, girl. What have I ever done to you?"

"Nothing. But you've never done anything *for* me, either." She pulled up a chair and spun it about, leaning over the back and staring at Jack. "What are you doing here, Señor?"

"Righting wrongs. Saving lives. Same as you. Only better."

Miles leaned forward, preventing Selena from responding with her usual sarcastic venom. "I get that you like being enigmatic but I'm not having it anymore. I think that whatever's going on out here might be a threat to the moon launch—and now it's looking like Dr. Evil might be involved. Those two things are serious enough that I'm not in the mood to be nice." He pointed a finger at Jack. "Who do you work for? I want specifics."

Jack seemed to weigh his options but finally he relented and said, "I work for The Gibbon. Have you heard of him?"

Miles and Selena exchanged a look and then Miles gave a nod. "A local legend, right? An immortal that supposedly became more than a man."

"That's right. Only he's no legend. He's real. I met him years ago when I was here on assignment. It changed me, Captain. After that, I decided to stay…these boys with me are part of his Jungle Patrol. They're locals that I trained in CIA techniques."

Selena downed her bourbon and slammed the glass down on the table. "Bull."

Jack frowned in response. "Girl, I've slugged men for calling me a liar."

"You're welcome to try and punch me—but there's no guarantee that you'll get your hand back."

"No one is punching anyone," Drake said. He tapped Jack on the arm, bringing the fellow's focus back towards him. "Let's say I believe you and you work for The Gibbon. What do you know about what's going on around here?"

"I suspect you know about the construction that's been going on but it's more than that—I've heard that it's a mining operation" Jack said.

"Mining? For what…?"

"That's the question, isn't it?" Jack ran a hand through his hair and said, "I haven't heard anything about Dr. Evil being around here but I do know that a blonde woman and an albino have been sighted in these parts. Maybe they're working for him?"

"No," Drake said. "I know them."

Selena noticed the way Captain Action's features drew tight when Jack mentioned the woman—she knew that it was Uliana Uliana that Jack was talking about.

Jack rapped the table with his knuckles. "There are men out here—professionals, with lots of heavy artillery. I know the man that's leading them, too. He's out of my past—a...protégé of mine named Rex. He's incredibly good at what he does but he's also cruel."

"Do you think he might be the mastermind behind all this?" Selena asked. "Assuming that Dr. Evil isn't really here?"

"No, Rex is a good leader of men but he's not the kind to supervise something massive—especially not if it's related to the moon mission. That's not his style at all."

"When can we meet The Gibbon?" Drake asked, surprising both Jack and Selena with the sudden change in topic.

"Why would you want to do that?" Jack inquired.

"For one thing, he sounds like he might make a good ally in all this. Second, how could I pass up the chance to meet an immortal?"

Jack sat back and smiled. "You don't believe me. You think I'm playing you instead of giving you an honest answer about my organization."

"Not at all."

Jack stood up and his men immediately rose, as well. "I'll send word to The Gibbon that you want to meet him but I wouldn't get my hopes up. He's not like you or I. He regards outsiders with enormous suspicion. It took years for him to accept me." He fixed Drake with a stare. "He's the guardian of the jungle and its people, Captain. If he thinks a man—or a woman—poses a threat to the sanctity of his realm, he won't hesitate to remove them."

Captain Action made no move to rise. He merely nodded and said, "I'm sure he'll be able to find us if he decides to speak to me."

"Yes," Jack agreed. "He will." He turned after nodding quickly at Selena and led his men out of the bar.

■ ■ ■

"The Gibbon isn't real," Selena said as she and Captain Action left the town. It was deserted now, the last of the evacuees having fled as the moon rose in the sky. "I've heard those stories since I was a little girl but I've never believed them."

Drake looked thoughtful. "There's something going on here," he said. "Is there really a man wearing the skin of a gibbon, living for hundreds of years? Maybe not. But I do think there might be someone out there using the name and the legend. Jack wasn't making it all up."

"And tell me again why we're not just sleeping the night in the town? We have our pick of beds."

"The water is tainted, remember?"

"So we don't drink it."

Drake grinned. "I'd feel more comfortable outside of La Primavera, Selena. The area's large and mostly unknown to us. There could be people hiding out in basements or alleyways all over town and we'd have no idea. By camping out in the open, I think we're more likely to notice someone slipping up on us. The jungle—even this one—is something I feel like I know. An unfamiliar town scares me a lot more, even if it's supposedly abandoned."

They returned to their jeep and Selena retrieved their camping equipment from the rear of the vehicle. She tossed some of it to Captain Action and said, "We have one tent and two sleeping bags. Think you can control yourself if we sleep next to one another?"

"I'll try my best," he replied in a deadpan voice. "We could always take turns standing watch."

Selena nodded as she helped Drake set up the tent. "If you think that's best, I'm game for it." She paused and then asked, "So how close were you and Uliana?"

"Getting a bit personal, aren't you?"

"That close, then?"

Drake sighed and drove a stake into the ground. "Yes. That close."

NINE: SABOTAGE!

Drake awoke with a start. He had been deep in slumber, dreaming that he and Uliana were once again confronting Dr. Evil in the bowels of the earth. This time, the villain was hanging on by his fingertips, barely avoiding a fall into a seemingly bottomless chasm. Drake was kneeling at the rim of the hole, one hand outstretched—his old foe was desperately trying to seize the offered lifeline but he kept failing to grab hold.

"Let him fall," Uliana had whispered in the dream—but Drake had kept trying to save the other man's life. When they finally grabbed hold of one another, Drake attempted to pull Evil back to the surface but the villain cackled in triumph and yanked hard, releasing his other hand's grip on the lip of the chasm. Both men fell, hands still clasped...dying as they had lived—together.

"Captain!"

Drake sat up, his senses suddenly on alert. That was Selena's voice—she was not in the tent with him, meaning that it was still her turn on watch... and something had gone wrong.

Seizing his sword and his hat, Captain Action burst from the tent. He saw Selena engaged in battle with two men, both dressed in black and wearing full facemasks that hid their features. The men both brandished machetes and had pushed Selena back up against the side of the jeep. She was skillfully fending off their blows with her dagger but even in the gloom Drake could see numerous cuts on her person, each seeping blood.

Captain Action felt a familiar tingle of excitement rush through him— these were the moments when he was most alive, when all the doubts and worries of the world were lifted from his shoulders. When situations became life-and-death, there was no time for recriminations or self-doubt—he had to give himself over to his training and his instincts, two things that had never steered him wrong.

Selena ducked under one of the machetes and stabbed outward with her dagger. The knife dug deep into her attacker's chest, just missing his heart...the man staggered away but he took her weapon with her as she failed to yank it free.

Concern was evident in her eyes as she realized she was now barehanded against her remaining foe—but at that moment salvation arrived in the form of a man wearing a yachtsman's cap.

Captain Action barreled into the big man with a lowered shoulder, sending him flying away from Selena. The masked man landed hard on his side but he was a professional because he rolled to the side and was back on his feet with impressive speed.

The two blades came together with a loud clang, the first in a flurry of blows that each blocked from the other. They moved together in a dangerous dance of death, each trying to gauge any weaknesses in the other man's style. Finding none, the masked man attempted to use his larger size to his advantage, swinging his machete with tremendous force. If he wasn't able to slip past Captain Action's defenses by normal means, he intended to use brute force to overwhelm the slightly smaller man.

Captain Action let out a grunt as he blocked each blow. The impacts each sent shockwaves of pain up his arm and into his shoulder but he refused to yield. The one downside to taking such powerful swings was that the motion caused the machete-wielding man's stance to open, exposing much of his torso…but that would only prove useful if Drake could find a way to take advantage.

Taking a chance, Captain Action made the dangerous decision to allow his defense to slip, revealing his left shoulder and upper arm to his foe—the action allowed the masked man to strike and he took advantage, driving his blade hard against the Captain's arm. Because he twisted at the last minute, the Captain was able to avoid a deep wound but he still felt searing pain as the machete drew blood in a superficial manner.

Simultaneous to this attack, Captain Action struck back, aiming his own sword at his enemy's exposed midsection. His sword slashed deep, its lightning design accentuating the pain as he yanked it free, tearing the edges of the wound.

The masked man howled and dropped his sword, using both hands to clutch at his bleeding side. He spun about and ran towards the jungle— Captain Action took off in pursuit but only got a few steps before he heard the familiar sounds of a helicopter. The wind around him began to kick up, blowing debris into his eyes. He stepped back as a bright spotlight momentarily shone down upon him and he realized with a chill down his spine that he was perfectly illuminated if the men in the helicopter held rifles.

Sure enough, bullets began to rip at the ground in front of him and

Captain Action spun back about and ran towards the camp. He saw that Selena was already crouching behind the jeep, returning fire with her pistol. He slid down next to her and the two of them ducked down as bullets ripped into their vehicle. The assault broke off seconds later and the helicopter sped off to the northeast.

Captain Action rose to his feet and confirmed his worst suspicions—not only was the man he injured gone but the one that Selena had wounded was dead, his body ripped apart by bullets.

"It's my fault," Selena murmured. "They were completely silent—by the time I realized they were in the camp, one of them had already cut the fuel line on the jeep." She uttered a string of obscenities in Spanish, only some of which Action was familiar with. She kicked one of the tires of the jeep—it was the only one not hit by bullets. "I must look like such an amateur, Señor."

"Don't beat yourself up over it. The best advice I can give you is to let the past be the past."

"That's hard to do when the past is staring you in the face."

Uliana.

Captain Action frowned as a lovely face framed by blonde hair appeared before his mind's eye. He began to examine the dead man, searching for any clues to his identity or employer. "Can the jeep be repaired?" he asked.

"Not out here," Selena answered. She had opened up the hood and was peering beneath. "We have three flat tires, a cut fuel line and it looks like several bullets struck the engine. Wherever we go from here, it's going to be on foot." She straightened and sighed. "I still feel like an idiota."

"Don't. These men aren't run-of-the-mill goons. They're well trained. I like to fancy myself a pretty good swordsman but that guy I fought was able to hold his own." Captain Action stood up, having found nothing in the man's pockets—no identification, no encrypted orders, not even a crumpled photograph of a girlfriend or lover. "Did you notice the direction that the helicopter went?"

"Si. To the northeast. We're on the right path, at least." Selena examined her numerous cuts and scrapes. "I have a first aid kit if you have any wounds that need tending."

"I have a superficial cut but I'll take some antibacterial spray—don't want anything in this jungle to infect it." He moved to her side and touched her shoulder. "Let me patch you up and then you can hit the sack. You haven't gotten a wink of sleep yet."

"And I'm not going to be able to!" she exclaimed. "I can sleep when I'm dead, *Señor*. We should pack up and move on before the trail is too cold. We can't be too far away."

He could see that he wasn't about to win any arguments with her in her current state so he merely nodded and set about using the first aid kit to treat their cuts. She hissed once or twice and he suspected that she might be hurting more than she wanted to let on. Their close proximity made his heart rate increase and he thought he detected something similar happening to her. Despite her repeated jokes about his age, he felt certain that she found him attractive—and there was no denying the feminine appeal that she held for him.

He cleared his throat and stepped back. There would be time enough after the mission to see if their attraction was real. It was dangerous to engage in such conduct in the field—not only did it create a distraction but it frequently led to hurt feelings. Men and women in dangerous situations often came together because of mutual shared experiences that created a false sense of intimacy. When things calmed down, they usually realized that they had little in common.

"How do you feel?" he asked.

She flexed her shoulders and rolled her neck. "Good as new."

"Then we'll pack up and head out—leave behind everything that's non-essential. We won't have the jeep to haul our stuff around."

Selena set about grabbing her things while Captain Action moved away and stared into the gloom. A well-trained killer…helicopters…a legendary jungle-man…this mission was quickly taking on a larger scope than he'd expected.

And, of course, there was the looming specter of Dr. Evil.

TEN: REX

Dawn was breaking by the time Drake and Selena heard the sounds of gunfire in the distance. It was a testimony to their bravery that they quickly picked up the pace and began running towards the sounds of battle, rather than turning in the other direction. By the time they got close to the conflict, they both held guns in their hands.

Drake motioned for Selena to crouch and she did so, joining him in peering around a set of thick trees. Just up ahead, something looking like World War III had broken out—and until Drake got a sense of who was who, he didn't plan to get in the middle of it.

There were two sides in the battle; that much was immediately obvious. One side was outfitted in battle fatigues and armed with state-of-the-art assault weapons—these men also wore familiar facemasks that hid their features, just as the two that had sabotaged the jeep had worn. The other side was more rag-tag in appearance and weaponry—the majority of these men were obviously locals and they wore uniforms that looked a lot like those sported by Jack Oat and his companions.

The two groups were totally oblivious to Drake and Selena—they were far too focused on annihilating each other. The jungle floor was lined with bodies, showing that one side at least was coming close to succeeding— the masked men were gradually winning, their superior firepower giving them the edge. In fact, Drake saw several of the opposition starting to pull back into the relative safety of the jungle—a full retreat was about to break out.

"No sign of Jack," Selena whispered. She had obviously recognized the two sides, as Drake had. "But I'm willing to bet that guy's the one he was telling us about. The one he used to mentor." She pointed towards one of the masked men and Drake nodded—while the rest of the troops were well trained, this man was obviously a step above. He pressed the attack, standing fearlessly at the front of his forces, ignoring the bullets that whistled past his body. He shouted orders to his men, refusing to let up even when it became obvious that his enemies were fleeing. A number of Oat's crew went down with bullets in their backs.

Another moment passed and then a sudden silence fell upon the bloody scene. The masked men had won, leaving only a handful of their enemies to escape. On the ground some of the wounded still moaned and writhed but these were quickly stilled by gunshots from the standing warriors—in some cases, they put down men from their own side.

The leader of the masked men removed his face covering and Drake stared hard at his features, trying to see if he recognized him from any international wanted posters. The cruel features and red flattop didn't ring any bells, however.

Captain Action looked at Selena. "Stay here. I want to talk to him."

"The hell I will," Selena hissed. "I'm not some American girl that you can try and protect—I'm my own person and a damned fine agent, Miles Drake!"

Captain Action grinned. "I was kind of hoping that you'd have my back by picking off anybody that looked like they were about to shoot me…but

The leader of the masked men removed his face covering...

if you're that offended by the suggestion, you're welcome to come with me."

Selena looked slightly chastened and then she broke into a grin. "Think when all this is over, I can be called Action Woman or Lady Action?"

"Sorry, but you'll have to make do with The Porpoise—either that, or wait in line for the Lady Action name to become available."

■ ■ ■

"Someone's coming."

Rex looked around quickly, having heard the warning from the man at his side. His eyes widened slightly at the sight of the two figures walking towards them, hands held up. One was a gorgeous young woman…but it was the man in the colorful uniform and yachtsman's cap that made Rex gasp. "Captain Action," he said, marveling at how bizarre the name sounded out loud.

Rex held up a hand to keep his men from opening fire and took a few steps towards the new arrivals. "This is quite a surprise," he said. "I had no idea that we warranted the attention of the A.C.T.I.O.N. Directorate!"

Captain Action and Selena paused about ten feet away from Rex. "Can we lower our hands? We're just here to talk," he said.

"Of course."

"I take it you already know who I am," Captain Action said. "I was hoping to find out who you were…and why you just slaughtered these other men."

"My name is Rex and we were minding our own business when The Gibbon's forces set upon us. We were just defending ourselves."

"Good thing you just happened to be armed to the teeth," Selena said.

Rex favored her with a crooked grin. "Lucky us."

Captain Action pulled the man's attention back to him by asking, "Why did your men sabotage our jeep?"

Rex's smile faded away as he answered, "We're involved in some important work, Captain. My men have standing orders to dissuade outsiders from interfering. They obviously felt that you and your lady friend might be headed into an area you didn't need to be in." He gave a shrug of well-muscled shoulders and handed his still-smoking rifle to one of his lieutenants. "Seeing the two of you, it becomes clear why we only had one man return—and he was in poor shape. Your reputation precedes you, Captain."

Selena cleared her throat. She raised her chin and asked, "I'm La Marsopa. Have you heard of me?"

Rex stared at her for a moment and then shook his head. "That means... dolphin? Fish?"

"Porpoise," she replied with a chilly tone.

"Ah. Well...No. Should I have?"

Captain Action spoke up before Selena could answer. He could see that she was embarrassed and a bit annoyed that Rex had never heard of Mexico's finest agent. "Who do you work for, Rex?"

Rex laughed, taking a moment to watch his men as they finished off the last of the wounded men. "I consider that information part of the mercenary-client confidentiality privilege—but I'll be more than glad to take you both to meet my employer."

Selena shook her head. "I don't think I'm interested in traveling with a man who kills his own people." She gestured to the corpse of the man that was just murdered. "That man could have been healed by any doctor worth the title."

"We travel light," Rex replied. "Every man knows the risks—if you're not able to walk under your own power, you're not able to come home. We do them a mercy by putting them down instead of leaving them to the animals and the elements."

"You call that...mercy?" Selena asked with shock.

"I do." Rex took out a cigarette and held it out for one of his men to light. "Now...it's not a particularly long march to my base. From there we can send word to my employer that you want to meet up. If we leave now, we can be there by the early afternoon."

Captain Action took one step closer to Selena. "I think we'd prefer to travel on our own. If you're not willing to give us the information, then we'll just find it on our own."

Rex took a drag off his smoke. "I don't think so, Captain." At a small signal from their leader, Rex's men pointed their weapons at Captain Action. "In fact, I *insist* that you come with us. If the girl isn't important to you, we can sell her to some of the locals along the way. If you're like me, you're probably sick of hearing her talk."

"Go to hell!" Selena exclaimed.

"After you, beautiful," Rex replied.

Captain Action looked at the assembled force—he and Selena were outnumbered by several dozen. Despite this, his voice was full of confidence when he replied. "If you don't lower your weapons and leave us alone, you're going to regret it."

"Really?" Rex asked with genuine curiosity. "And what makes you think that?"

With incredible speed, Captain Action's hand dropped down to his waist—he seized not his gun or his sword but instead a small rectangular device that was small enough to fit in the palm of his hand. It was mostly featureless though it featured a depression in the exact center of the device. He held it over his head so that everyone could see it clearly. His thumb rested lightly over the depression, ready to press it. "This is alien technology, discovered by the Directorate back in '65. One press of this button and every one of us will die in a small-scale atomic explosion."

Several of Rex's men shifted uncomfortably but their commander merely sneered. "You seriously expect me to believe that? That looks like a garage door opener."

"You want to take that chance?"

Rex looked over at Selena, who looked somewhat concerned by the turn of events. Her own eyes kept flicking to the device that Captain Action held in his hands. "Show us," Rex said, obviously deciding that Selena didn't look quite frightened enough for him to believe that death was only a button push away.

Captain Action suddenly smiled and it was such a cruel expression that Rex was momentarily taken aback. "With pleasure." He pushed the button lightly and the device began to hum. The sound grew in volume until it made Rex wince. "Once activated, I'm the only one that can disable it. We have about sixty seconds so if you're a religious man, I'd start praying."

"You're seriously going to kill yourself over this?" Rex shouted, visibly annoyed as several of his men broke ranks and started to run.

"Death isn't the same for me," Captain Action replied. "In fact, I've died several times—the Directorate keeps a steady supply of clone duplicates in alien-created tubes. They'll just wake up the next in line."

Rex's jaw clenched and he waved at his men, ordering them to lower their weapons. "Turn it off, damn you."

Captain Action took Selena by the hand and bolted towards the jungle. "I'll do that once we're safely away from you, Rex. Don't try to follow us!"

Rex watched them go, the humming sound fading into the distance. He whirled about, snarling at his chief lieutenant. "Let's get out of here—if you see any of the men that just ran, shoot them."

"What about Captain Action?"

"We don't have to give chase. He's going to come to us—I guarantee it."

■ ■ ■

Drake and Selena kept running for well over a mile, heading northeast as much as possible. When they finally slowed down, neither of them was panting very hard—they were both quite fit and used to such exertion.

Drake pressed the switch on the device, silencing the hum. He saw that Selena was staring at him with a mixture of awe and confusion. Sensing her question, he tossed the device to her and said, "It's just a noisemaker. Doesn't do anything else."

Turning the device over in her hands, she asked, "You carry this...why?"

"For the same reason I carry a flare—there are times when you want to share your location and don't want anyone to miss you. Trust me, if I'd pushed that button twice as hard, it would have gotten twice as loud. Nobody will miss you when you're using that."

"So...you were bluffing? What if they'd decided to just shoot you?"

"Then I'd be dead."

"So...no clones?"

Drake shook his head. "No. I made that up, too." He looked at her curiously. "You're familiar with cloning?"

"Only from old pulp fiction magazines. It's like swapping people's brains—it's not real. It's *la ficcion*."

Drake grunted. "Real life is stranger than any pulp fiction magazine, Selena. The stories I could tell you..."

Selena handed him back the noisemaker, a look of admiration in her eyes. "If you weren't so old, I think I'd be in love, Señor."

"I'm not that old," he replied testily. He instantly regretted it because she broke out into a huge grin when he did. "Not that I care if I'm attractive to you or not," he added.

She nodded in agreement, though her eyes said that she saw right through his protests. "Of course not, Miles. Anyway, we're much too professional for such distractions."

She picked up the pace, moving ahead of him. Captain Action found himself very aware of the swaying of her hips and he couldn't shake the feeling that she was deliberately putting an extra wiggle in her walk.

ELEVEN: KAWIL

The strain of the past night and morning began to take its toll on both Selena and Captain Action as the day stretched on. Moving through the thick brush, with the summer sun beating down upon them, caused both to become sluggish and increasingly short-tempered. When they suddenly came to a watering hole, both came to an unspoken agreement to take a break.

Captain Action removed his cap and ran a hand through his sweaty mane. His uniform was designed of a unique fabric—it trapped just enough of his perspiration to cool his body without making him so uncomfortable that he chafed. Despite this, he was still irritable, finding Selena's continued attempts at humor to be more annoying than funny.

Selena sat her rump down on a large rock and pulled out a canteen of water. She had tied up the front of her shirt to just below her breasts, revealing a flat stomach that glistened with sweat. She saw Drake walking along the edge of the water, examining it, and said, "I wouldn't drink from that. It's probably full of all sorts of nasty things."

"I wasn't planning to—but there is something in the water that caught my eye." He stripped off his gunbelt and backpack, tossing them aside before wading out into the water. He made it far enough he was waist deep before plunging his hands into the water. They came back with a backpack, which he drug to shore.

Selena had slaked her thirst but she was still tired. As such, she remained seated and asked, "I don't think it's any better than the one you already have, Miles. If you were thinking of upgrading, I think you made a mistake."

Captain Action ignored her as he dropped to his knees and opened the soggy backpack. He dumped out its contents and began rifling through them. He picked up a compass and examined it closely. "That's what I was afraid of," he murmured.

"What is it?" Selena asked, motivated enough by the emotion in his voice that she left her comfortable perch and joined him.

"A Soviet-issue compass. I've seen it—and this entire backpack—before. It belonged to Juthrbog." He stood up and looked around, studying the ground for any signs of recent tracks. While he spotted numerous ones that belonged to animals, there were no human ones to be seen. "He wouldn't have discarded it like this...."

Selena knew what he was thinking and she abandoned her usual jocular tone when replying. "I'm sure Uliana is fine, Miles. There are no signs of a struggle here—no blood, spent cartridges or bodies."

Drake didn't respond, instead stopping where he stood and cocking his head to the side. Selena imagined he was thinking of all sorts of grisly scenarios in which his lost love and her companion might have met their ends. She sympathized and was about to say so when things took an unexpected turn.

The Captain suddenly lunged for the belt he'd tossed aside before wading into the water. He dropped into a roll, plucked his pistol out of its holster and was back up in a crouch even before Selena had realized what was happening. "Get down!" he shouted.

Selena's battle-honed reflexes saved her life. She hit the ground as soon as Drake's warning had reached her ears and the motion was all that prevented a spear from embedding itself in her upper body. Instead, the implement of death hit the ground beside her, its sharpened edge easily piercing the earth.

Hearing the tell-tale clacking sound of Captain Action's pistol charging, she retrieved her own gun just in time to see several tribal warriors emerge from the jungle, each armed with spears or knives. These men wore little in the way of clothing—shin guards and loincloths being all that kept them from being naked. Their bodies were painted like that of a jungle cat, with orange-tinted paint and cheetah-like spots. Each of them had shaved their heads, leaving only a small portion of hair in the center that was pulled into a topknot.

The men attacked with incredible fury, one of them striking Selena's wrist with the end of his spear. The blow was enough to knock the gun from her hand and send pain rocketing straight into her brain. Before she knew it, the man had the point of his spear shoved against her throat.

Captain Action, meanwhile, had discharged his unique weapon. The shot hit one of the men running towards him, sending him flying off his feet and into one of his companions. Before he could get a second attack off, the Captain found himself surrounded by knife-wielding warriors, each of whom seemed eager to decapitate him.

"Enough!"

The warriors paused but none lowered their weapons. Captain Action knew he could take out several more if he kept up his own attack but then he'd be overwhelmed...and then the truth of what had happened to Uliana and Juthrbog would go unanswered.

A man strode forward. He was dressed and painted similar to the others but this one wore bracers on his arms and had additional painting around his neck and shoulders—a field of black that made him look like he was wearing a collar of sorts. "Drop your weapon, Man of Action."

Drake hesitated but finally did so. The gun landed between his legs and stayed there. He eyed the newcomer boldly and said, "If you know who I am, then you must know that I'm not an enemy that you want to make."

"It seems that you have made that decision for me," the man replied. "We were watching as you talked with the one called Rex. He is no friend of ours."

"Then you must have also seen his men draw guns on us—and our escape."

"Yes. That's the only reason you're not dead." The man dipped his head slightly. "I am Kawil, named after the god of power. I am chief warrior and advisor to The Gibbon. If you wish to live, you will take your woman and leave this place. Dark forces have been loosed and I believe we are in the days spoken of long ago—the days when we as a people shall either come to an end or prove our ultimate worthiness to the gods."

Selena rose slowly to her feet, keeping her eyes on the man holding the spear to her throat. "I'm getting really tired of having people ignore me so they can talk just to you, Miles."

Despite the situation, Captain Action smiled. "Next time, we can trade places."

"Promises, Señor."

Kawil looked from one to the other and shook his head. "Neither of you fear death. That is impressive…but also foolish. Will you listen to me and flee? I have no wish to see your names added to the list of the dead."

"I appreciate that," Drake replied. "If you work for The Gibbon, then you must know Jack Oat?"

"Yes. He has lived among us for many years."

"We saw some of his men fighting Rex's forces a few miles back—it looked like they took a lot of losses. I believe that Rex is possibly working for an old enemy of mine. If that's true, you're not going to be able to win this battle…not without help. If you'll take me to The Gibbon, I might be able to trade information that will help both of us."

Kawin waved a hand and spoke to his men in a dialect that Drake didn't recognize. They lowered their weapons and backed away. "The Gibbon does not like outsiders. They cause us nothing but trouble."

"I can't leave until my mission here is done. As a matter of fact, the sooner I finish my job, the sooner all these outsiders in the jungle will be gone. You have my word on that."

"Then I will take you to The Gibbon…but if he tells you to leave, that is what you must do. His word is law in these woods. To disobey him is to court immediate death. Do you understand?"

"Clearly." Kawil and his men turned, obviously intending for Captain Action and Selena to follow—they paused when Drake asked, "Do you know anything about the man that owned this pack? He would have been traveling with a woman with yellow hair."

Kawil nodded. "Yes. They were led through here by Rex's men. The pale-skinned man argued when one of the men was rough with the woman. They hit him in the head with the butt of a rifle and tossed his bag into the water. Then they dragged his body along after them. This was some time ago."

Captain Action's eyes flashed with anger and his expression became quite dark—Selena had never seen the likes of it from him before and it chilled her somewhat. He looked like a man possessed and she was suddenly quite glad that she was not one of his enemies.

TWELVE: JUNGLE LORD

The trek to The Gibbon's lair was a winding affair, obviously intended to confuse the newcomers and prevent them from locating it easily without assistance—Selena and Drake were led into a small village in late afternoon, when the day seemed exhausted and was ready to cede its power to the night.

The village was an interesting mix of modern and traditional—men dressed in ceremonial garb walked side by side by camouflaged soldiers armed with pistols. Women and children watched from the sides of the dirt paths, regarding Captain Action and Selena with open distrust.

The people lived in small one-room houses made of wood and mud but here and there Selena spotted hilarious signs of the modern world: one house had a "No Solicitation" sign nailed to the front door while a young girl wore a small pin fastened to her clothing that read *THE BEATLES!*

The procession led by Kawil paused when a little boy ran into their midst. The youth was no more than six or seven years old but he stared at Captain Action with wide eyes. He pointed at the symbol on the Captain's chest and shouted in Spanish, "El Terror Negro!"

Drake smiled and knelt in front of the little boy. He tapped his symbol and replied in perfect Spanish, "No, I'm not The Black Terror. You have comic books here?" When the little boy nodded, Drake said, "I used to read about his adventures too. Very strong!" He made a muscle and let the little boy feel it. "But I'm no superman like The Black Terror...I'm called Captain Action. I'm a man just like anyone else."

"Armed with alien technology and trained in every fighting art known to man," Selena reminded him. "Not quite just like anyone else."

Drake chuckled but kept his gaze focused on the little boy. "I mean that everything I do, I'm able to do because of hard work. You can train your body to become something amazing—and you don't need Formic Ethers or anything else to make you strong." He ruffled the young man's hair and stood back up, finding that Kawil was watching him closely. "Sorry for the delay," he said.

"It is fine," Kawil replied. "El Terror Negro is very popular with the young people. When Jack Oat first arrived, he had a box full of comic books and pulp magazines. The children still read them, even though they are falling apart by now."

"What about you?" Selena asked.

Kawil blinked in confusion. "What about me?"

"Did you read them, too?"

"Yes. I have read them. Some of the stories are outlandish but they do stir the blood."

Selena reached out and touched Captain Action's arm. "This man is like those heroes. He inspires people. He does good work. You should listen to him, not try to force him away. If there's one person in the world that you can count on to save your people, it's him."

Captain Action kept his expression neutral but he felt flattered by her words. She usually spoke with a slightly sarcastic tone to her words, as if she always wanted you to doubt her sincerity—but none of that was present now. She meant what she was saying.

Kawil seemed to sense the truth that lay behind her words, as well. He nodded and said, "I have no doubt of that, Señorita. But we serve The Gibbon. He is our protector and our eternal champion. It is for him to decide which paths we are to take."

Selena nodded, letting her hand drop from Drake's arm. "And if he says we're to be kicked out of the jungle, you're going to go along with that?"

The painted warrior turned away, his words drifting over his shoulder. "If he says to kill you both on the spot, then I'll do it without hesitation."

■ ■ ■

The Gibbon's private lair was a cave, set into the base of a large stone wall that served as the edge of his people's property. There was something odd about the shape of the cave's mouth and the smaller, shadowy indentions above. It was only when they were about to enter that Captain Action realized what it was; there was something like the skull of a gorilla in the shape of the entrance.

"This is The Gibbon's Mouth," Kawil said. He paused outside the entrance. "Step inside and you will see The Spirit That Stirs, the Eternal Champion."

Captain Action started to move forward but Selena held back, noting that Kawil was stepping away from the cave. "You're not coming with us?"

"No. It is for you to speak to The Gibbon. Convince him to let you stay and all will accept his ruling."

Selena followed Drake into the dark cave, her body tensed in case this was a trap. For a moment she could see little in the dim lighting but suddenly torches flared to life, illuminating the room so brightly that she was momentarily blinded. A throne dominated the circular room, a torch burning on each side of it. In the chair sat a masked man, his upper face hidden by a domino-style mask with white eye-coverings. He wore a dark green and black uniform covered by a cloak of gibbon fur. His exposed skin was heavily bronzed and a neatly trimmed beard framed a firmly set mouth.

Despite the ludicrous attire, there was something strangely noble about the man and Selena's normal desire to make light of any situation was quelled. She moved to Drake's side, their hands so close that they were almost touching.

The Gibbon spoke first, his voice a booming thing that seemed to reverberate off the surrounding walls. "You were told to leave my woods."

"Yes," Captain Action confirmed. "We can't do that, however. Mankind is on the brink of sending men to the moon…and whatever's going on out here might pose a threat to that."

"I don't care about the moon—I care about my people and this jungle.

The strangers that have come here have killed innocents and they must pay. Your presence will only complicate matters."

Selena spoke up. "Your people are outmanned and outgunned. Let us figure out what's happening and we can call for backup. When things are over, we'll all leave and you can go back to pretending to be a living phantom."

The Gibbon stared hard at her. "You doubt my powers?"

Selena crossed her arms in front of her and nodded. "I definitely doubt that you gained immortality by putting on an animal skin."

"None of that matters," Captain Action said. He cast a warning glance at Selena, silently asking her to stop antagonizing The Gibbon. Their jobs would be a lot easier if they could get the masked man's assistance and he hoped that Selena realized that. "What's important is that we have overlapping goals. Rex and whomever he works for poses a threat to your people—and to ours. We can join forces to remove them from the jungle. Then, like Selena said, we'll leave you alone."

Rising from his seat, The Gibbon crossed over to stand right in front of Captain Action. He towered over Miles Drake by several inches but Selena noticed that the jungle lord's boots sported lifts—without them he would have been eye-to-eye with her partner. "I can sense that you are a man of honor, Captain…but I have made a sacred vow to protect this place. I don't need your help nor do I want it. You were asked nicely to leave—continue to refuse and you will be escorted out by force."

The two men stared each other down for a long moment. It was Captain Action who first looked away, saying, "You heard the man, Selena. Let's go."

Selena blinked in surprise—she would have bet a month's salary that the Captain wouldn't have backed down for anything. She found herself hurrying after him, leaving The Gibbon in his cave. The torches snuffed themselves out, plunging the jungle lord back into darkness.

"Miles!" she said, having to jog to catch up to him. She saw Kawil watching them briefly before entering the cave. "Slow down, please."

Captain Action did so but he kept walking, obviously wanting to exit the camp quickly. "They're going to take us back to town, Selena. We need to be on our way before then."

"Maybe we should."

"What are you talking about?"

"We came out to look into rumors of something odd being done in the jungle—we've confirmed that. We've discovered that some jerk named Rex is leading a paramilitary force…that a former CIA agent has trained and armed a bunch of locals to resist them…that some lunatic is pretending to be The Gibbon…that Dr. Evil might be involved somehow…and that there's a former Soviet soldier and your ex-girlfriend on Evil's trail. We need to go back and report all of this. It's beyond just the two of us now."

"I'm not going back."

"You're letting your feelings for this Uliana overwhelm your common sense!"

Captain Action stopped and turned towards her, his face completely expressionless. His eyes, however, were full of fury. "I'm on a mission."

"Si, you are—to make sure that the moon mission launches without a hitch. Saving your ex-girlfriend and her current lover isn't a part of that!"

"They're not lovers."

Selena stopped in place, her lovely lips suddenly twitching into a smile. "Do you hear yourself? Even now you can't stop yourself from defending her honor."

Captain Action sighed, putting his hands on his hips. "Maybe this is where we split, Selena. You go back and contact the authorities and I'll push on. I know what you're thinking but this really isn't about Uliana—whatever's going on out here is big. Maybe it's related to the moon mission or maybe it's not. Either way, it's something that needs to be stopped. Whoever Rex works for knows you and I are on the case—that's probably going to speed up their timetable. They've moved their location once already, remember? We can't lose them again."

"If that's what you want," Selena replied. Captain Action saw the hurt and anger in her face but there was nothing to be done about it. "On the way back, I'm going to see if I can find Jack—I think he knows more than he's let on. If nothing else, he can give a lot more detail about Rex and how much of a threat he might be."

"That's a good plan."

Selena nodded and began walking away, splitting off from Captain Action. "I hope you find her, Miles."

Captain Action started to deny the implication of her words but he bit his tongue. Further denials would only strengthen her conviction. Instead, he shouted after her, "Be careful!"

Without a further word, he resumed his trek towards the Northeast—this time, it was a solitary one.

THIRTEEN: MINING OPERATION

Captain Action was grateful for the sweat-absorbing properties of his suit. Without it, he would have been drenched and miserable—but with the suit doing its job, he felt more refreshed than he would have otherwise. Even so, his canteen was starting to get low and he would need to find more provisions soon.

He tried to focus on keeping his senses alert but he kept thinking back to the things that Selena had said: was he compromising his mission because of concern over Uliana's safety? It would be hard to deny that he'd done so in the past—heck, he'd gotten reamed out pretty good for going off the grid in Japan when he'd come to believe that Uliana was out there in the grip of Dr. Evil. He'd been proven right, even uncovering a mystery that probably wouldn't have been found out otherwise if not for his actions but that didn't change the fact that he'd disobeyed orders.

The sounds of heavy machinery and male voices suddenly interrupted Drake's reverie. He sped up, using his sword to slice through the thick undergrowth. He came to a cliff, lying down with his belly on the ground and inching towards the edge. Down below he saw something that made a smile form on his face—he'd found it. The site of whatever operation was going on in the jungle was right before him.

In the far distance, he could see open water but his focus was riveted to the men right below. This was obviously some sort of mining or drilling camp, for he could see heavy machinery digging into the earth.

The camp was in a deep valley, one that looked like it had been formed untold years ago. The drop from the cliff to the bottom of the valley was easily several hundred feet and it was approximately six football fields across in length. Drake couldn't fathom what natural event had formed this depression and he was sure there was no man alive in the area that would have known, either.

Most of the men in the camp were manual laborers but a few of Rex's

The site of whatever was going on in the jungle was right before him.

armed forces could be seen, watching over the operation. None of them seemed very concerned about any dangers coming from the jungle though the soldiers snapped to attention as Rex emerged from one of the many tents set up around the perimeter of the camp.

Rex shouted orders to some of his men and they hurried off but the distance and the tumult from the machinery prevented Drake from hearing the man's words.

Narrowing his eyes, Drake scanned the camp slowly, looking for any sign of prisoners. He saw none but he did see odd equipment here and there—some sort of glass apparatus with sharp points that were embedded into the ground near some of the past drilling spots. The glass occasionally glowed a rich purple in color before fading and Drake got the distinct impression that something was being drained from the ground and absorbed into the apparatus. The technology seemed out of sorts with Rex and his men…but it was perfectly in keeping with the alien-inspired tech belonging to Dr. Evil.

There was suddenly a tumult down below and Drake turned his attention to a dark-skinned man that was running through the center of camp, holding something against his chest. Whatever it was, the object was wrapped up in a towel or cloth.

Rex reappeared, guns now holstered on each hip and a rifle slung over his back. A crowd gathered around the military leader and the man with the cloth and Drake hurriedly opened up his backpack and pulled out a small directional listening device. He turned the business end of the device towards Rex and heard the following exchange:

"What the hell's wrong with you?" Rex asked.

"You must tell the master that this is it! The energies were already so rich that we suspected this was the proper site but there's no denying it now— one of the drills broke off a piece of the rock and I've been studying it. This is it! This is the site of the extinction event!" The man unwrapped his prize and Drake squinted. It looked like he held some sort of pitted rock… and suddenly a memory fell into place. The Captain had seen something like this before—and recently. Pablo had taken him to Sky Rock, which was near the original site of the mining operation. Sky Rock had been a meteorite, part of a larger piece of rock…and from the scene he was witnessing now, Drake was positive that the full meteor was below the ground in front of him. Its impact must have been what caused the deep depression.

Captain Action heard footsteps behind him and he quickly backed away from the cliff and stood up. One of Rex's men had come into view, carrying a rifle casually at his side. The masked man was whistling, having not noticed the Captain yet.

Drake sprang into action, sprinting towards the masked man. The gunman spotted his attacker at the last moment and attempted to raise his rifle but the weapon was kicked out of his hands by Captain Action's right foot.

The masked man was well-trained and recovered quickly. He shot a hand towards Drake's throat, putting all of his weight behind the move. He flexed his fingertips, forming a wedge that could have shattered the Captain's windpipe.

Drake sidestepped the fatal blow by a mere inch, feeling the snap of air as the masked man's hand sailed past him. The action gave the hero a momentary advantage and he took it, knocking aside the man's wrist with a palm-heel strike and then seizing his forearm and pulling him closer.

The masked man's momentum made it easy for Drake to spin him past, exposing the mercenary's back. The Captain drove a cocked elbow into the base of the man's spine, sending a lightning bolt of pain straight into the man's skull.

The soldier fell to his knees, moaning in pain, and Drake grabbed the man's right arm in both hands. He gave a mighty twist and the sound of a bone cracking in two reached Drake's ears. Releasing the ruined limb, Drake delivered a quick punch to the base of the man's skull, sending him into unconsciousness.

After dragging the man back into the jungle and tying him up with a small rope from his backpack, Captain Action returned to the cliff. Rex and the man that had brought him the chunk of space rock were nowhere to be seen but his keen eyes spotted someone else of interest: someone that he had hoped to never see again.

The man striding confidently through the camp wore a Nehru jacket, sandals and a large golden amulet that hung low on his chest. His longish blond hair fell straight down his back and he sported a moustache and forked beard. This was Dr. Stefan Tracy, known before his transformation as "the hippie guru of engineering."

Of course, it was all a lie now…Dr. Tracy had been transformed into Dr. Evil and his very appearance had been altered. What Drake was looking at now was nothing more than a plastiderm disguise. Evil's skill in manipulating the disguising material was second only to that of Captain Action himself, making it easy for him to impersonate almost anyone on earth.

The disguised Dr. Evil ducked into one of the small huts, disappearing from sight.

A part of Drake wanted to climb down into the camp right now and tear the madman out of that hut. He wanted to beat the man into submission, making him reveal what his plans were and what had happened to Uliana. The greater part of his mind pointed out the danger of doing that, however—without even Selena to back him up, he'd be cut down in seconds.

Drake moved back into the jungle, his mind racing. If Selena made it back to town and summoned help, it would still be a day or two before they would arrive en masse. That was too long for him to wait and he certainly wasn't going to make the trek back to civilization, not when his arch-foe was so close at hand.

There was only one option: he had to return to The Gibbon and use this new information to convince the jungle lord to help Captain Action launch an immediate assault on the mining camp.

Picking up the pace, Captain Action vanished into the undergrowth—now that his worst suspicions had been confirmed about Evil's involvement, he knew that whatever was going on here, it posed a threat to the entire world. No more doubts or recriminations—from here on, Drake's purpose was clear: stop Evil and save Uliana. Nothing else was a suitable outcome.

FOURTEEN: SECRETS

From the outside, Selena Rubio's life looked perfect.

She was the third of four children—the only daughter of a wealthy businessman. She grew up in a large house with a pool out back and several servants that catered to her every whim. Precocious and beautiful, Selena was doted upon by her father and the expectations for her were immense: she would grow up and marry someone of equal or better social standing, potentially making the family fortune double or even triple.

She heard her father's stories at every family gathering—how he had risen from the streets to this incredible success. He did it through hard work and determination, he said. 'Never give up,' he told his children. 'See that brass ring and don't let anything stop you from grabbing hold of it.'

She was proud of him, proud of her family's name and proud of the way the other children seemed so in awe of her home. Despite the fact that he refused to let her into the business side of his life, he allowed her to train with the family bodyguards. They found her quite adept at learning how to fight, shoot and move with stealth. It was all great fun to her and the men seemed to regard her as a particularly bright pet, never knowing that their lessons would one day shape her life in surprising ways.

In addition to her physical training with the bodyguards, she found that she loved the water. She took to it like a fish, gaining the nickname La Marsopa for the way she seemed at home in the sea or in the pool. She swam so often that she sometimes felt ill at ease on dry land.

Life was good and she had every reason to believe that it always would be—having known nothing but peace and happiness, why would she suspect anything else?

But there were cracks in that façade of family bliss. Her father brought the boys into the family business at an early age but Selena was kept on the outside, her gender a barrier to the truth about what her father did for a living. She caught bits and pieces along the way, hearing snatches of dialogue about deliveries and shipments, as well as the occasional visits from foreigners in dark suits.

The day after her sixteenth birthday, a group of six armed men burst into the family compound, killing the bodyguards and servants. They took the family hostage while their leader interrogated Selena's father in another room. She heard the man asking about missing shipments and receipts that appeared to have been doctored. She realized for the first time that her father was not in traditional exports/imports—her father was a drug lord.

The knowledge had hit her with all the impact of a freight train. Her family's success hadn't been merely built on the back of 'hard work,' it had been built through the despair and suffering of others. His father's drugs had found their way into Selena's school and she'd seen friends ruined by the stuff…and she suddenly remembered hearing whispers and seeing frightened glances from her teachers when her father would visit the school. She'd thought they were intimidated by his wealth and success… but it was more than that. They knew he was dangerous.

When one of the gunmen made an attempt at molesting her, Selena fought back. She broke his nose and took his gun. While her brothers and mother screamed, she opened fire, killing the men that held her prisoner. In the next room, the man with her father panicked…before she could break in and save the man she had idolized for so long, his life had ended. The leader of the drug squad had shot her father in the forehead, blowing his brains out all over the recently repainted wall.

Something snapped in her at that moment. She threw down the gun and launched herself at the man that had not only murdered her father but who had removed the veil from her eyes, exposing the awful truth behind her life. The man had shot her in the right shoulder but she honestly hadn't even realized that until hours later when she'd come out of shock at the hospital. She'd apparently beaten the man to death with her bare hands.

It was the very next day when a man from the government had appeared at her hospital room. He said that the officers that had first arrived on the scene had described her actions and, while he knew that she must have been suffering greatly, he had a job offer for her: serve her country while making up for the sins of her father.

She'd agreed without hesitation.

■ ■ ■

A soft rain began to fall and the sun drifted behind thick brown clouds. Selena tilted her face up to the sky, letting the water strike her face. The drops were cold but they felt good—it had been too long since she'd been swimming and the rain felt like a lover's kiss against her skin. Running both hands through her damp hair, Selena realized that despite her appreciation for the rainfall, she might need to find shelter if the drizzle became a storm. Otherwise, she'd probably end up with pneumonia, given how long she still had to go before reaching town.

"You're a woman after my own heart."

Selena whirled about, drawing her pistol in one smooth motion. She peered into the gloom, ignoring the rain that dripped into her eyes. The rain came harder now, a rumble of thunder punctuating the sense of danger that she now felt. "Who's there?" she demanded.

How quickly her life could go from one of relief to one of potential death…!

"No need for that," a man said and this time she recognized his voice. Jack Oat moved into view, dressed in his jungle fatigues and hat. "It's just me," he said with a smile. He wore a backpack and he slipped it off his shoulders and reached inside. He tossed her a hat and she caught it with one hand. "You might have a use for that."

Placing it atop her head, she said, "Thanks." She holstered her weapon, favoring Jack with a small smile.

"You're welcome." Jack moved closer to her, slinging the backpack over one shoulder as he did so. "Where's the good Captain? Did he abandon you?"

"We had a difference of opinion about how to proceed," she admitted. "I was hoping to run into you—I'm going back to town to report in and summon some additional support."

"Did you see The Gibbon?"

"We saw a man dressed up like him."

Jack grinned. "Still not a believer, eh?"

Both of them jumped as another crack of thunder boomed across the jungle. The rain was really coming down now and Selena felt obliged to shout her next words. "There are no such things as ghosts, Señor Oat."

"Then how do you explain the fact that the people around here have reported seeing The Gibbon for hundreds of years?"

"He's a man wearing a mask. He could be anyone."

"I suppose he could. Why were you hoping to see me? It wasn't because you were taken with my handsome face, was it?" He started walking with her in the direction of civilization.

"Your *fantasma* told us to get out of the jungle, refusing our help. If you've worked for him for any length of time, you must know what kind of resources he has. Can he really stand up to Rex and his men?"

"He's done incredible things," Jack replied. "Rex has the advantage in terms of weaponry and the size of his forces but The Gibbon knows this land and his men will follow him to Hell and back. Loyalty trumps the mercenary spirit of Rex's people."

"Loyalty won't stop bullets."

"Where's Captain Action gone? You mentioned that you had an argument…he decided to ignore The Gibbon's warning?"

"He went on without me," she said with a shrug.

"I'm sorry to hear that…of course, I'm pretty sure that you were told to go home and let The Gibbon handle it. Instead, you're planning to bring more outsiders into his woods. Both of you disobeyed me."

Selena stopped suddenly, looking at him. The rain slowed to a light drizzle, the storm coming to an end as suddenly as it had begun. "Disobeyed you?"

Jack nodded and then his left hand shot forth. The backhanded blow would have caught a normal person square in the face but Selena's battle-honed reflexes allowed to quickly raise an arm. She blocked the worst of it, though the strength behind the attack was enough to numb her entire side. Before she could recover, he spun around and struck her from behind, knocking her to her knees. He followed with a quick punch to the base of her skull.

"*Madre de dios*," she muttered, her head buzzing.

Her right leg flew out and caught Jack's ankles. She tried to knock him off balance but she was in an awkward position and his bulk allowed him to foil her attempt.

Instead, he grabbed her by the hair and yanked her head back. He opened his mouth to say something but Selena clasped both fists together and slammed them upward, catching him on the mouth. His lower lip immediately began to swell and he released his grip on her hair, staggering back a step.

Selena fumbled for her gun but she couldn't make her fingers close around it. She looked up at Jack, just before he delivered a final punch that sent her into dreamland.

"I hate to hit a woman," Jack said. "But you're an exception—you're so dangerous, you're practically a man."

When he was sure that she was out cold, he bent down and lifted her up in his arms. "This is for your own good," he whispered—the words seemed more for his own mental well-being than for anything else.

FIFTEEN: PLEA FOR HELP

Miles Drake moved through the jungle, keeping his senses on alert. The rain and the thick clouds overhead reduced visibility and he was constantly looking about to make sure that none of Rex's men had spotted him.

He hoped that Selena had made it someplace warm and dry. He felt a bit bad for how they'd parted but he remained convinced that he'd made the right decision. The facts that he'd left the mining camp at all showed that he wasn't being foolish with regards to Uliana…though a part of him had wanted to stay behind and try to rescue her he was able to use sound judgment in realizing that he couldn't do it alone.

He needed The Gibbon.

■ ■ ■

Scouts alerted the camp to his return long before he actually arrived. Kawil was waiting for him outside with arms folded over his heavily painted chest. "You were told to leave the jungle," the priest stated.

Captain Action elected to ignore that statement. He walked right up to Kawil and stopped less than a foot from the other man. "I need to see The Gibbon."

"He has already given you an audience," Kawil replied. The man's jaw was clenched tightly and Drake could tell that the man was angered by his refusal to accept The Gibbon's decision. "I would be well within my rights to have you killed on the spot, Man of Action. Your presence here is an affront to The Gibbon's rule."

A small crowd had gathered to watch the scene, many of them obviously anticipating that Kawil was going to give the interloper a swift smackdown. Captain Action lowered his voice and said, "Kawil, you're smarter than this. You know damned well that Rex has your people outgunned. You also know that Rex isn't the man in charge of their operation—I just confirmed who Rex is working for and he's the most dangerous figure in the world. Take me to see The Gibbon. I'll do whatever I can to help him save face but it's imperative that he hear me out."

Kawil's upper lip curled upward but he spun about and gestured for Captain Action to follow him. The priest's bare feet sank into the mud as he walked and Drake looked at the sky, grateful that the rain had ceased. He wasn't one to pin his hopes on omens but it felt like a good sign that the weather was starting to improve.

Kawil instructed Drake to wait outside The Gibbon's cave and the priest dipped inside. He remained there for nearly five minutes, leaving Drake to ponder his next action. He wasn't concerned about being able to convince The Gibbon that they needed to unite—he was certain that he'd be able to do that, given the masked man's stated desire to protect the jungle. Rather, he was concerned about how to make sure that Uliana would be safe when they staged their raid on the mining camp—he hadn't actually seen her so he had no idea where she was being held.

He refused to even consider the fact that she might be dead. Dr. Evil would have recognized her and surely he would have thought her more valuable as a pawn to use against Miles than as a corpse.

"He will see you," Kawil said, stepping back out of the cave. The priest stopped Captain Action by touching his arm as the agent started to move past him. "He is not pleased that you have returned."

Captain Action nodded and suddenly asked, "Tell me the truth, Kawil… who is he?"

"He is the same man that he has always been—our sovereign protector." Kawil squeezed the Captain's arm for emphasis. "It is important that you accept the things that your mind resists. Your so-called civilization wants everything to fit into small boxes, easily classified. The world is far too strange for that."

"Believe me; I'd never argue that point."

■ ■ ■

The Gibbon was seated on his throne when Captain Action entered, the torches on the walls of the cave repeating their process of lighting when Action reached a certain part of the room. He wondered how it worked—dismissing the possibility of something supernatural, it could easily be accomplished with wires and pressure plates but that seemed like a stretch considering he was in a cave in the middle of the Yucatan.

Then again, it seemed just as likely as the notion that The Gibbon was an immortal warrior.

"You and your companion should have heeded my words," The Gibbon said. Even with the torches burning, he was still cloaked in semi-light, adding mystery to his appearance. Captain Action noticed that The Gibbon's leather boots were caked with mud, indicating that he'd been out of the cave recently.

"She listened to you," Captain Action said. "Hopefully she'll be back in town soon enough."

"No," The Gibbon thundered in reply. "She did not. I told you both to leave here and allow me to handle the situation. Instead, you sent her back to summon more help while you deliberately disobeyed me by continuing on into the jungle."

Captain Action's eyes narrowed suddenly. "You've seen her, haven't you? That's the only way you'd know that she was going to report back in. And it explains the mud on your boots."

The Gibbon paused before replying. When he did, his voice was softer than before, as if he realized that he was coming off as the villain here. "Yes, I have spoken to her. I made it clear that I did not want more agents coming into these woods."

"She wouldn't have changed her mind about what to do," Drake said. "So you probably had to stop her with force." His right hand clenched into a fist. "Am I right?"

The Gibbon stood up. With the lifts in his shoes, he was able to look down at Drake, saying, "She is unharmed. But, yes, she is here at the camp."

"I want to see her."

"I'll take you to her—but I think you wanted to try and convince me to help you? If so, this is your chance. What have you discovered that will change my mind?"

Drake frowned for a moment but then he focused on his mission. Selena's well-being would have to wait, no matter how much it frustrated him. "The mining camp is digging for some sort of giant meteor that must have crashed here millions of years ago. What they're hoping to do with it, I don't know—but that's the point of all this. Dr. Evil is the mastermind behind it all. I've dealt with him before and he lives up to his name."

The Gibbon stroked his chin and nodded. "I've heard of him. You saw him yourself?"

"I did."

"Then perhaps you're right. My only priority is protecting my people and if Dr. Evil is here, then it would be foolish of me to turn away the help of a man that's fought and defeated him many times."

Captain Action felt himself relax and realized that he'd been bracing for the worst. "We need to organize your men and strike before they realize I'm on to them."

"Give me twenty minutes and I'll have an army ready to march."

"That's fine—and that'll give me a chance to check in on Selena."

Captain Action added a slight tone of warning to his words. Allies or not, he wasn't going to be happy if he discovered that his friend had been brutalized.

The Gibbon placed a hand on the Captain's shoulder and gave it a firm squeeze. "Your loyalty does you credit."

"You're an American."

The Gibbon quickly removed his hand and stepped back, the shadows lengthening about him as he did so. "That's ridiculous. I was born here and I have protected this land for countless generations."

"No, that's not true. When we first met, I took your skin color to be that of a local but up close, I can see that it's been bronzed from years in the sun. Given that—and the presence of a well-groomed beard—I think I have a pretty good idea about who you really are. The question is: Why?"

The Gibbon paused before speaking. "The legend of The Gibbon has some truth to it, Man of Action. The mantle has been passed from father to son for many generations. When I met the last of the line, he was desperately trying to have a son…but there was something wrong with his plumbing, I suppose." The masked man shook his head. "He was fearless. His only concern was the well-being of his people. You wouldn't believe how long it took me to convince him to let me enter his jungle in pursuit of an escaped criminal. He finally agreed but only on the condition that he accompany me every step of the way. He…didn't make it back."

"What happened to him?"

"That…is a tale that's a bit long in the telling."

"I think we might have time," Captain Action replied.

The Gibbon stared past him, obviously looking back into the mists of time. "Some of what I have to tell you was given to me by Kawil, some by my predecessor…and some of it is guesswork on my part. I'm confident I've got the bulk of it down, though."

He began speaking, his voice carrying the tone of one reciting a myth. The Captain felt himself drawn into the moment, the images being painted before his mind's eye taking shape with each passing moment.

■ ■ ■

Several years ago

Deep within the Yucatan jungles lay a cave of wondrous design. Mother Nature had, through centuries of rain and wind, shaped the cave's entrance so that it resembled nothing less than a humanoid skull, its mouth forming the entrance to the lair within. The local tribes dubbed this cave 'The Gibbon's Lair,' for it was said to be the abode of a man who had lived continuously since the late 1400s when a local hunter had discovered a gibbon that was unlike any other—the man had forged some sort of spiritual connection to the beast and when it died, it conferred its strength and cunning to its human friend.

The hunter became The Gibbon, striking at all those that threatened the sacred jungle through greed and evil. He stalked them like a hunter would track his prey and eventually brought them to a violent sort of justice.

In the years since, The Gibbon had adopted the cave as his private residence. Though the natives attributed his constant appearances over the years to immortality, the truth was that he had married a woman while visiting family in a nearby town. She had come home to the cave with him and bore him a child. Their son had eventually become the second Gibbon and through the years more descendants had done the same, all operating with the same weapons and attire—a fearsome set of furs, leathers and domino mask.

The current Gibbon was the 22nd in the line and he was as young and fit as his father and his father before him. But his greatest attribute was the keen mind he possessed, which allowed him to outthink enemies of all types.

In the section of the cave dwelling that he used as his library, The Gibbon now sat before a mixture of herbs that were slowly burning, their smoke enveloping his masked face. The part of his features that was not hidden by his mask was lined with wrinkles, evidence that he was not a young man.

Elsewhere in the home his daughters and granddaughters were cleaning up after dinner. Because there had never been a female Gibbon, he and his wife had tried repeatedly for a son. A woman dressed in The Gibbon costume would doubtlessly destroy the legend of an immortal jungle protector...it would become clear that the most recent Gibbon had not in fact been the original but rather just the latest in a long line. And the legend had power, no doubt of that. Thus, a son was needed before it was too late...but increasingly, that time seemed to have passed. His wife had died many years before and he'd refused to take another, despite the protestations of his daughters and his advisors.

Already, the Gibbon could feel old age looming over him...he would grow slow and inevitably die. There had to be someone to follow in his footsteps....

The Gibbon sighed, pushing such dark thoughts away. He looked around his home and smiled. Despite the fact that he lived in the jungle, the Gibbon kept a well furnished abode and was relatively comfortable. His children sometimes accompanied him on journeys to the so-called "civilized countries" but what they had seen only confirmed that their father was right to spurn the Western nations in favor of his jungle home. Because of his advancing age, it had been several years since he had last visited the towns and cities within reach of his home.

The Gibbon leaned into the mist, breathing it in. The scent was like roasted almonds with just the faintest hint of alcohol in its wake. The herbs allowed him to expand his consciousness, sometimes seeing into the near future or recent past. If the stories he had heard were true, then the

The Gibbon leaned into the mist, breathing it in.

outside world was wracked with more wars, civil unrest and something called "rock and roll." The old hero needed to know more if he was going to protect his people.

The Gibbon's head jerked as images flashed before his mind's eye. The images came in spasmodic hits, like still photographs being illuminated on a moving wall. He saw a man dressed in unusual attire, a skintight bodysuit of various shades of blue…an odd sort of cap upon his head… and a tri-colored symbol upon his chest, the English letters CA present in the center.

The Gibbon saw the man engaged in battle with a bizarre individual that looked inhuman…a figure with an exposed brain and blue skin. The two of them were fighting against a background of pure black, as if their location was unimportant to the vision. What The Gibbon needed to know was that these two men were important to the future of his people…but why? And which, if either, was a friend? Confusing the vision even more was the slow appearance of the sacred furs, lying on the ground between the combatants. The furs were soaked in blood.

The scene shifted, the two strange men no longer seen in the smoke. Now he saw the moon, hanging heavy in the sky. It was a bloody moon, its surface covered by a sheen of scarlet. Slowly the moon's face began to change, until it almost resembled that of the blue-skinned man with the exposed brain. The man was smiling down at the earth and The Gibbon felt the ground rumble beneath his feet.

Now he was standing in the midst of his village, surrounded by dead bodies. Men, women and children all lay in brutal, broken heaps. He looked down at himself and realized that he was naked, his old body lined with scars. He fell to his knees and his body began to break down, the skin turning leathery before crumbling into dust. Then even his bones began to decay and he saw his own skull fall to the jungle floor, where a wind blew earth over it. Within moments, there was no trace of himself or his people.

■ ■ ■

The images seemed to fade away from The Gibbon's field of vision, leaving him alone in his library. His heart was hammering in his chest. He felt like he understood the visions now—the man with the blue skin and exposed brain posed a threat not only to The Gibbon's people but to the greater world as well. The white man in the "CA" uniform was opposed to him, though that didn't necessarily mean that he would be a friend to The Gibbon.

If left unstopped, all of this would lead not only to the death of the villagers but the end of The Gibbon legacy.

He rose and left his room, hurrying outside. The rumble of thunder made the ground shake around him. Without even bothering to tell his daughters where he was going, he sprinted through the jungles, finally coming to a small camp located less than a mile from his cave.

The man known as Jack Oat was standing in the center of the camp, a tin cup filled with coffee in his right hand. The man was looking up at the sky, obviously trying to gauge how severe the coming storm would be.

Oat heard The Gibbon's approach and his hand automatically dropped to the pistol he wore in a holster on his hip. When he recognized The Gibbon, he smiled and relaxed. "Hello, my friend. Can I get you some coffee?"

The Gibbon paused, breathing heavily. Though still in great shape, he was no longer capable of physically exerting himself the way he could even just a few years ago.

Jack Oat had come to the jungle just a few months ago. At first, The Gibbon had tried to persuade him to leave…but gradually he had come to understand that the man posed no threat to his people. In fact, he could help them greatly by giving them knowledge of the outside world.

Oat was what was known as a "secret agent," though The Gibbon found the term confusing. If he was a "secret," why did he announce that fact?

The man had come to the jungles in pursuit of bad men but he had found them with The Gibbon's help and put them to justice. He had remained in the Yucatan, never explaining why—but The Gibbon felt he understood. Jack Oat was adrift in life, having lost his purpose. He was seeking a new way of living and he admired what he saw in The Gibbon and his people.

"Is Kawil still nearby?" The Gibbon asked, not bothering to respond to the offer of a beverage.

Oat nodded. "Kawil! Your boss is here."

Kawil emerged from one of the tents that were set up around the campfire. The Gibbon knew that Kawil had been spending a lot of time with Oat, reading Black Terror comic books and looking through copies of *Life* magazine.

Kawil had been the village's chief warrior for some time and had only recently ascended to the position of advisor. He wore bracers on his arms and sports several new tattoos and skin paintings that identified his new role within the village. The field of black around his neck and shoulders still looked odd on him but The Gibbon believed he would grow into the job—he had a quick mind and a good heart. The Gibbon had even considered making Kawil his heir to The Gibbon legacy but he valued the young man's current role too much to risk it.

"Is something wrong?" Kawil asked, obviously concerned.

"I have had a vision."

Kawil placed a hand on The Gibbon's arm and lowered his voice. "What did you see?"

"Two men, battling to the death. One of them posed a threat not just to the jungle but to the entire world…but I saw myself dying, along with all our people."

"Thought you were already a ghost," Oat murmured with amusement.

Kawil and The Gibbon ignored the jibe. "The visions are meant to warn you of danger. You can change the future."

"Not this time," The Gibbon replied. "I am too old."

"Nonsense!"

"I can feel the weight of years in my bones. I carry a burden that makes me weary."

"Then let the belief of your followers give you strength," Kawil said.

Oat cleared his throat. When The Gibbon turned to him, he said, "I have a suggestion—I know of a weapons cache not far from here. Some of the guns belonged to those men I rounded up, some of them were ones I brought with me. Your people stand a better chance of protecting themselves from outsiders if they're armed with modern materials. I can take you there and let you have them. Hell, I'll even teach your people how to use them."

The Gibbon considered this for a moment. "Perhaps you're right. In this new era, our traditional weapons may not be enough." He looked hard at Oat. "Are you running from something, Jack? Is that why you are still here?"

Oat nodded and turned away. "Yeah, I'm running away from something…but I can't get away 'cause I see it in the mirror everyday. I've done bad things and trained some guys that have done even worse."

"You cannot change the past but it is never too late to begin a new tomorrow."

"Spare me the platitudes, please." Oat moved to start kicking dirt onto the fire, snuffing it out. "So do you want the guns or not?"

The Gibbon seemed to weigh his options before he replied, "I feel that your presence here is not an accident. You are destined to play a great part in whatever is to come. So, yes, I would like to see this cache of weapons."

■ ■ ■

Kawil had not been happy when The Gibbon had told him to return to the village. He revered the jungle hero, of course, but he no longer believed him to be infallible—working in close quarters with the man had taught him that. The Gibbon *was* immortal but not in the way that most believed. He was an idea and that could never die, not so long as men and women believed in it.

Kawil stepped through the foliage, moving with such stealth that a Brown Brocket Deer grazing nearby never took notice of him. Had he been in the mood to hunt, he could have killed the beast with the dagger he wore at his waist…but this was not such a night. His mind was awash with thoughts concerning the outside world, ideas put into his head by the magazines that Oat brought with him. The man was coarse and Kawil was never sure if he was being honest with the villagers but he found himself drawn to him nonetheless.

He saw the lights of the village up ahead and knew that he would come across one of the posted sentries soon. At times, he would attempt to sneak past them to test their effectiveness but tonight he was to return with haste, as per The Gibbon's orders.

Something suddenly caught his eye and he stopped in place, his body going tense. He crept forward, confirming his suspicion—it was the body of a dead gibbon, lying on its back with one long limb tossed across its chest. It had died recently, for the stench of death was not yet present and the jungle's insects had yet to claim the body for their own uses.

This was a bad omen and Kawil looked back in the direction of Oat's camp. His first instinct was to take off in search of The Gibbon, to both warn and protect him.

Perhaps this was a test, he mused. A test of his faith and his loyalty… in the end, he must trust in The Gibbon. He would do as he had been told, to return to the village and keep the people there safe. He would put his belief in The Gibbon…and he would pray.

■ ■ ■

The trek to the weapons cache took nearly three hours and the night was nearing its end by the time they reached their goal. The first glow of the rising sun was visible on the horizon and the nocturnal animals were quickly giving way to the early risers that preferred the daylight hours.

"Stop," The Gibbon said. He had followed Oat in silence for the most part, his thoughts occupied by his disturbing vision.

Jack Oat ceased hacking his way through the undergrowth. He took one look at the grim expression on his companion's face and instantly tensed for danger. The Gibbon knew his surroundings in an almost supernatural manner—Oat prided himself on his acute senses but The Gibbon put him to shame in the jungle.

"What is it?" Oat asked, using a kind of stage whisper.

"When did you last visit here?"

"Two or three weeks ago. Why?"

The Gibbon gestured towards the grass just in front of Oat—someone in heavy boots had been through here recently. Not only that but they'd cut away some of the undergrowth to speed their journey. In the dark, neither man had noticed that the going was easier than normal.

"You have good eyes," Oat murmured.

"The ground gives up its secrets willingly to me."

"Right." Oat sheathed his machete and drew a handgun from the shoulder holster that he wore. He studied the ground again and said, "I count three sets of tracks."

"Agreed." The Gibbon moved past the American, his head tilted to one side. "Three voices ahead. All men." In a slightly harsher tone, he asked, "How much are they paying you, Jack?"

Jack Oat slammed the butt of his gun against the back of The Gibbon's skull. He repeated the attack twice more before The Gibbon slumped to the ground.

With his heart hammering in his chest, Oat wiped his mouth with the back of a hairy hand. "Not enough, old man. Not enough."

■ ■ ■

The Gibbon woke up to a world of hurt. His skull felt like a jaguar had decided to repeatedly pounce upon it and when he opened his eyes, his vision was blurry enough that for a moment he was unable to accurately count the number of men standing in front of him. When things finally coalesced into a clear view, he saw Jack Oat with three others, all of them dressed in denim pants and dirty shirts. They were local thugs, of the sort that would harass and rob tourists to survive. Occasionally they would venture out far enough to become a concern for The Gibbon but most of them knew to avoid the jungles.

These three would need reminding, it seemed.

A small pickup truck was parked nearby, backed up against a small hovel that looked like it had been hastily built amidst the trees. Through the open door, The Gibbon could see the guns and ammunition that Jack Oat had promised to deliver to his people.

The Gibbon tried to move without attracting attention. His back was against a thick tree and his arms were tied behind him, looped around the trunk of the tree. The bonds felt sturdy but he felt certain that given enough time he could work his way free.

"Looks like *el invitado* is awake," one of the men said. He was the obvious leader of the three, with an oily mustache and thinning hair. The Gibbon gauged him to be in his early fifties with years of violence in his background. He was still fit but beginning to spread a bit with middle age—his two companions were younger and, judging from the size of their eyes, a bit awestruck to be in the presence of the legendary Gibbon.

Jack Oat avoided meeting The Gibbon's gaze. "Just hang tight, Gibbon. I'll cut you loose when we're done here."

The Gibbon ignored the three thugs, keeping his attention fixed on Oat. "What is happening, Jack?"

"He's got a bad habit," oily-hair said with a sneer. "And I help him manage it."

"Shut the hell up, Francisco." Jack stepped up closer to The Gibbon and lowered his voice, "I won't let them kill you. All they want is the guns... and your furs."

The Gibbon's eyes narrowed sharply. "That is like telling me all they need is my soul. You know the sacred nature of these furs, Jack. I will die before I let them be taken from me."

"They're just monkey skins," Jack replied hotly. "Go and kill another one—nobody will know the difference."

"If that's true, why do they want mine?"

Francisco put a hand on Jack's shoulder, ignoring the glare that the former CIA operative gave him. "I can answer that one. You've pissed off a lot of dangerous people and disrupted more than a few smuggling operations—there's a huge price on your head." Francisco pretended to think of something, his expression becoming one of mock realization. "But you know, Jack has a point. If we bring back some smelly old furs, who is to say if they were really yours? We need more proof. Like, I'm thinking, we might need to cut off your *cabeza*."

"That wasn't the deal," Jack said with venom in his voice. "Don't try to screw me over, Francisco."

The barrel of a gun pushed hard against the side of Oat's head. His eyes flicked over to see that one of the younger men had drawn his weapon while Francisco had been talking.

Francisco was enjoying the moment, grinning from ear to ear. He poked Jack hard in the chest. "Don't mess with me, *hombre*. We've gotten what we need from you so there's no reason why we couldn't just put a bullet in your head and leave you here to rot, si?"

Oat appeared to considering his odds when he finally held his hands up and backed away. "Just give me the drugs. That's all I want."

Francisco snorted. "All you addicts are just the same. You talk a big game until you need your next hit and then you are nothing but a *cobarde*." He turned away from Oat and gestured to the man standing nearest the weapons cache. "Start loading the guns into the truck."

When the other man jumped to work, Francisco reached over to Jack Oat's side and drew out his machete. He held the sharp blade up into the morning sun and whistled as its surface gleamed. "Nice one, *amigo*. Good for hacking through limbs...and necks."

The young man holding the gun swallowed hard and asked, "Are you sure about this, Francisco? What if his ghost follows us out of the jungle?"

"You don't believe that *basura*, do you? It's all fake. Garbage! Look at him!" Francisco pointed at The Gibbon. "He's an old man that dresses in a mask and rotting furs. He probably gets some sort of kinky thrill out of it, that's all."

"I pity you," The Gibbon said. "All of you."

Francisco sighed and reached up to rub a spot between his eyes. "And why is that, Señor? Because we're all motivated by greed? As opposed to, say, wanting to run about in the jungle and screech like monkeys?" He laughed and sauntered over to The Gibbon, placing the machete blade against the hero's throat. The Gibbon seemed unfazed by the imminent danger. "When I was a kid, I heard the stories about you. They said you were immortal and invincible. I believed that bunk. I thought that someday you'd swing your way into town and help *mi familia*. But you never did. My father blew his brains out. My mother became a whore. All my brothers did whatever they could to survive...and so did I. So don't dare look down on me, Señor. I am what I am and I don't hide it behind a mask."

"It is not too late to change," The Gibbon said. "There is a good man inside you. I've seen it in your eyes."

"You are a fool," Francisco hissed. "You don't know the first thing about me!"

"I wasn't talking to you."

Francisco blinked in confusion—then he looked at Jack Oat and grinned. "I think he means you, amigo. He still doesn't get it, does he? You sold him out, just like you've sold out your whole damned country. All these guns were meant for your G.I. Joes, right?"

Jack stared at Francisco, his eyes slowly traveling down the man's arm, over the machete and then onto The Gibbon's calm face. "Right."

Francisco turned back to The Gibbon. "You see? He knows who he belongs to."

The Gibbon said nothing as Francisco spat on the ground and then pulled his arm back. This was the moment that would make Francisco a legend in the criminal community, the time when he was the one to bring down the fearsome specter that stalked the jungle.

Only that moment never truly came.

With an animalistic roar, The Gibbon flexed his arms, the tendons in his neck standing out as he strained. The bonds gave way, ripping apart, and the hero brought both fists against the sides of Francisco's skull. The boxing of his ears made Francisco squeal in surprise and pain. The machete swing went awry and The Gibbon neatly ducked under the attack, punching twice in the man's stomach.

The fellow that had been holding the gun to Jack's head was momentarily stunned by the sudden turn of events. This allowed Jack to strike. The former CIA agent knocked the pistol aside and then grabbed hold of the man's arm. He yanked it out straight and then drove an elbow down hard atop it, snapping the bone. The fellow screamed and dropped the gun. Jack didn't go for it immediately, instead choosing to punch his opponent in the throat. The man gasped and then was mercifully sent into unconsciousness by a follow-up roundhouse that knocked him back on his heels and then to the ground.

The goon that had been loading up the truck had somewhat faster reflexes than his compatriot. Before Jack had even broken the man's arm, his fellow criminal had realized the danger he was in. He set down the rifle he'd been putting into the bed of the truck and seized hold of a box of ammunition. He was loading shells into the gun when Oat turned his attention towards him.

Realizing that he was about to be in a very bad situation, Oat responded instinctively. He didn't have time to go for the fallen pistol before the rifle would be pointed in his direction so instead he grabbed hold of a large rock that lay between his feet. Ducking down and grabbing it, Oat came back up and threw it in one fluid motion—the rock sailed with unerring accuracy, striking the thug on the temple. The man staggered back, blood beginning to emerge from the cut that had been left behind. He swayed on his feet and then toppled over, groaning in confusion.

Oat took his time retrieving the fallen gun, pushing it into the waistband of his pants. He looked over at The Gibbon, who was standing over the fallen Francisco. The would-be crimelord was still breathing but his nose was broken and blood was flowing freely down his face.

The Gibbon took a step towards Oat but stopped abruptly when the CIA man held his gun up, the barrel pointed directly at the jungle lord's chest.

"Don't come any closer," he warned. His hand trembled slightly and The Gibbon could see that he was deeply conflicted.

"Are you really a drug addict?" The Gibbon asked.

"I'm not an addict." Oat sighed. "Look, I'm sorry. They said they wanted to take your furs and offered me enough to keep me going for another six months. I figured they could have the guns, too. I didn't know they were planning to kill you."

"Would you have done it anyway?"

"No!" Oat swallowed hard. "I respect you, I really do...but c'mon, the whole story about you being an immortal is bull and there's nothing special about an animal skin."

"That is where you are wrong. I *am* immortal. The man within these skins may die but The Gibbon remains...there will always been someone that picks up the mantle. I have struggled with that in recent times, thinking that because I did not have a son, I might be the last...but I won't be. There are others out there that can protect my people, perhaps better than I can. Those people I saw in my vision are coming and I do not have the knowledge of the outside world enough to truly recognize the dangers they might pose. But you do."

Oat lowered his gun, looking suddenly very tired. "What the hell are you talking about? You're asking me to stay on and do what Kawil does... give you advice?"

The Gibbon patted the furs that he wore. "When a man wears these, he becomes more than he was. He becomes the living embodiment of a dream. He is empowered not just by the spirit of the original Gibbon but by the hopes and desires of the people. If you truly want to find redemption, then these will help you."

"You're not making any sense," Jack replied. "I...I'm just a washed-up agent with a drug habit. You're talking like...like I'm going to be playing dress up in that monkey suit."

"You are. You will be the next Gibbon."

"What makes you think that?!"

"Because I am about to die…that is why we are here. This moment is where both our lives have led us." The Gibbon began to strip off the sacred garments that he wore. He let them fall to the ground, not stopping until after the mask was also removed. He wore only his furred briefs and boots.

"You're not about to die," Oat replied, growing increasingly uneasy.

"Yes. I am." The Gibbon stepped past Jack, turning his body towards the criminal that was now standing near the truck. Though still dazed from the rock to the head, the man had recovered enough to rise, pick up his rifle and take aim.

The gunman fired and despite his blurred vision, the bullets struck The Gibbon full in the chest. The jungle lord's body shielded Jack from the shrapnel and Oat shouted in disbelief as The Gibbon sagged to his knees.

Oat raised his pistol in retaliation and fired, blowing apart the bad guy's head. The corpse spun about and landed with a thud atop the pile of guns in the rear of the truck.

Oat sank down beside The Gibbon, catching him in his arms. *"Why did you do that?"* he asked angrily. "You have people that rely on you!"

The Gibbon smiled, blood beginning to bubble up from between his lips. When he opened his mouth to speak, his teeth were stained red. "Now they rely upon you. Take care of them, Jack. I believe in you."

Oat saw The Gibbon's eyes become glassy and his breathing ceased. This was the first time he'd ever seen the man without the mask and he was startled by how normal he looked. The Gibbon had always seemed taller and more vital than this fragile old man that Oat now held.

For several minutes, Oat remained where he was, holding the dead man's body. When he realized that Francisco was beginning to stir, he softly set The Gibbon's head on the ground and stood up.

He started to put a bullet into Francisco's brain but that didn't feel quite right. It wouldn't be enough to simply kill these three men, when they had robbed the world of The Gibbon. In a way, they would have still won…but there was one way that Francisco and his cohorts could be beaten.

■ ■ ■

Francisco groaned. He reached up to gingerly touch his shattered nose and he winced as the pain increased. He spat out blood and phlegm that had accumulated in his mouth and struggled to his feet. The first thing he saw filled him with concern: one of his men lay near the truck, his head lost in a mass of blood and brain. He quickly looked about to find his second man still alive, but tightly bound by jungle vines. A sock had been shoved in the man's mouth but his eyes were wide with fear and concern.

Francisco staggered forward, his foot bumping against yet another body—the man lay facedown on the ground, a pool of blood spreading out from beneath him. He wore Jack Oat's clothing and Francisco had no reason to suspect that it wasn't actually the ex-CIA agent. Obviously, he'd missed a good bit while he was drifting in and out of consciousness…but where was The Gibbon?

"Looking for me?"

Whirling about, Francisco looked for the source of the words…and he finally spotted The Gibbon, perched up in one of the nearby trees. Something about him looked different but in his dazed and worried state, the criminal didn't think too hard about it. "So you got loose," he said.

"I did. And your men killed Oat."

Francisco shrugged, trying to emphasize his bravado despite the fact that he looked like a bloody mess. "Good. Nobody will miss him, eh? Besides, now you and I can share the rewards and don't have to worry about him."

"You don't really think I'm going to join in on your little criminal enterprise, do you?"

"No…not really." Francisco looked about for a weapon but saw none. "So how are we going to do this? I'm not going down without a fight."

"I hope not." The Gibbon gestured towards the jungle. "Run."

Francisco hesitated for only a moment before he burst into a sprint. He leaped over the body of his still-living compatriot, ignoring the way the man shouted from behind his gag. Francisco was out for himself and no one else mattered.

Jack Oat smiled, feeling like a new man…but it wasn't he that jumped from the tree and set off in pursuit of his prey.

It was The Gibbon.

■ ■ ■

The frightened man was hardly at home in the jungle. He was a city boy, the sort that would venture out into the wilds to smoke dope, sleep with someone else's girlfriend or drink beer with his friends.

And, of course, to conduct illegal gunrunning activities.

But he was hardly familiar with the terrain, something that put him at a disadvantage when fleeing from The Gibbon. Though the man beneath the mask was now Jack Oat, the former CIA agent had spent a good period of time living out here and he was familiar with similar environments from a lifetime spent in dangerous situations.

Oat felt revitalized as he chased after the thug—whether it was something innate in the furs or simply the feeling that he'd been reborn as someone new, Jack hadn't felt this vital in years. Not since before he'd lost his faith in his mission and been betrayed by Rex.

A smile spread over his face as he followed Francisco deeper into the jungle. The man was loud, breaking branches and stumbling with nearly every step. It was hardly a test of Jack's tracking ability to keep up with him.

Francisco burst through a thick section of foliage and came to a sudden halt—he had inadvertently found a large cliff that ended several hundred feet above a rapidly flowing river. He looked down and saw jagged rocks extending above the water, making it hardly safe to leap downward, even if the distance had been shorter.

"You've run far enough, Francisco."

The criminal turned around and stared at his pursuer. The Gibbon was stepping towards him, not out of breath at all. "You…you're not him. You're Jack, aren't you?"

"You saw Jack's corpse, Francisco. I couldn't be him…not unless I'm a ghost. A specter who walks…just like the legends say about The Gibbon."

Francisco took a step back, his voice beginning to quaver. "We can work this out, amigo. You come work for me and I'll make sure you're never without a fix. I'll keep you supplied with drugs and girls. More than you could ever want! *Comprende*?"

"That's quite an offer," The Gibbon replied. "But it's not good enough. My people cry out for justice."

"These are not your people, gringo! You're a white man!" Francisco's voice was becoming more strident with every step that The Gibbon took towards him. "If you kill me, my gang will hunt you down! Your life won't mean anything anymore!"

The Gibbon smiled coolly. "That's where you're wrong. Just a few minutes ago, my life might have been meaningless…but not anymore. Thanks to you, I've got a new lease on life and new responsibilities." The masked man threw his head back and unleashed a strange, bestial cry. It rang out through the jungle and was answered by the calls of the true gibbons that lived amidst the lush foliage.

Francisco jumped when he heard the inhuman sound. He took one more step back…and it was one step too many. His foot found no solid footing, for he had moved over the edge of the cliff. His arms flailed and for a moment he felt renewed hope as The Gibbon lunged for him, attempting to grab his arms to save him.

Unfortunately, The Gibbon's fingertips just missed Francisco's sleeve and the killer tumbled away, screaming as he fell all the way down to the river below. His body struck a large rock and bounced away, vanishing beneath the water.

The Gibbon watched for a moment more, waiting to see if Francisco came back to the surface. All he saw was a streak of red being pushed downstream.

Turning away, The Gibbon planned out his next actions. He would bury his predecessor's body and then drive the truck into town, leaving the surviving criminal behind for the police. The man would tell the story of The Gibbon's continued survival and the legend would continue. Then The Gibbon would take the weapons to 'his' people. Kawil would know that he was Jack Oat, of course, but he had a feeling that the warrior would understand that he had become more than he was.

Jack Oat had been a flawed human being but he'd always wanted to be something greater. That's what had led him to the CIA and then to freelance work on the side. Something had always been missing and that emptiness had led him to loose women, alcohol and drugs.

All of those things would become part of his past, however. He had found something to assuage that desire for purpose. He was, now and forever, The Gibbon. He would protect these people as his own because they were his family, his friends and his responsibility.

The Gibbon smiled.

■ ■ ■

Miles Drake was silent for a long moment. He could understand better than most how a man could lose himself in a role, seeking a deeper responsibility than his old life had provided.

"You've never thought about giving up the role to someone else and returning to your old life? What about your family? Friends?"

"I have those things here, in abundance. I've taught them some of the outside world because they need to know to protect themselves but I've also tried to maintain their traditions. Their ways are so much better than

... the killer tumbled away, screaming as he fell...

ours, Captain. If you stay here for any length of time, you'll learn that. Hell, you might decide you don't want to leave."

"I'm...glad you've found a home for yourself." Captain Action rubbed his chin. "I wish that I could tell you that I think your people are going to be able stay safe out there but the world's getting a lot smaller every day. You won't be able to keep to yourselves for very much longer."

"Look around you, Captain. I'd say that we lost that hope some time ago."

"Good point. When all this is over with, you'll have to let me know if there's anything your people will need to help protect the village. Even if the Directorate won't help directly, I can always do something on my own. I'm sure your people need medicines and supplies, don't they?"

The Gibbon started to reply when Kawil burst into the cave. The priest fell to one knee just as the sounds of gunfire and screams began to fill the air.

"Gibbon!" Kawil gasped. "We are under attack! The man called Rex is here!"

Captain Action drew his pistol and was tensed for battle before Kawil's words were fully out of his mouth. He emerged from the cave, stepping out into the carnage.

The scene was one of pure horror—Rex and his squadron of killers was swarming into the camp from all sides, guns firing. Bullets ripped through men, women and children as The Gibbon's people struggled to find safety and locate their own weapons.

The cry of The Gibbon rang out, freezing everyone in place. Even Rex paused, seeking the source of the inhuman sound.

The Gibbon burst forth from the cave, his mighty thews pumping as he ran into the midst of the carnage. He brushed past Miles Drake, anger evident in the flexing of his muscles and the hard set of his jaw.

Less than a step behind was Captain Action. Miles matched The Gibbon's in both fury and speed—the horrors of war were bad enough when they came to the so-called civilized world but here, in what should have been a jungle paradise—the sin and greed of criminals seemed all the worse.

SIXTEEN: EVEN LEGENDS DIE

The distinctive charging sound of Captain Action's lightning gun was lost amidst the clamor of war. The unique weapon could only be fired three times before it needed charging but if used smartly, that was often all that was needed.

The Gibbon was headed straight for Rex and the Captain's initial intention was to follow suit—but when he heard a child's scream of terror, he instinctively whirled about to see what was happening. He recognized the same little boy that had earlier confused him for being El Terror Negro—but now the boy's features were contorted into an expression of pure terror. He was standing outside a small hut that Drake assumed was his home—it was now burning brightly and a woman lie at the boy's feet, bleeding from her shoulder. Drake thought she was still breathing but she was losing blood quickly.

Captain Action gave no thought to his own safety. These were the moments that gave his own life meaning. It was here, when instinct took over, that he strangely felt most at peace.

Bullets tore through the ground at the child's feet but he was too frightened to seek cover. The Captain dropped into a sliding crouch, aided by the muddy terrain. He streaked past the little boy, grabbing him by the waist. The duo came to a stop on the other side of the hut and Captain Action gripped him by the shoulders, staring hard into his eyes.

Speaking in Mayan, Captain Action said, "I need you to be brave—like El Terror Negro! I'm going to bring your mother to you and I want you to stay with her. Can you do that?"

The little boy nodded, wide-eyed. He flinched every time he heard gunfire but he was obviously resolute in following Captain Action's orders. Miles felt certain that if this young man could make it to adulthood, he was destined for great things—perhaps he'd never be The Gibbon but someday Kawil would need a replacement and Captain Action hoped that this youth might have a chance to fill that role.

The Captain waited for a pause in the conflict and then he was on the move, creeping out to the fallen woman. He seized her by the arm and dragged her back behind the hut—she was dead weight but again the mud made the action somewhat easier than it would have been otherwise.

Kneeling next to her, Captain Action pulled out a small first aid kit from a pouch on his belt. He deftly examined the woman's wound, locating the bullet still lodged in the meat of her shoulder. Digging in with his bare fingers, he was able to pull it free, tossing it aside and then disinfecting the area with a special spray. He didn't have time to sew up the hole but he seized a piece of gauze and took the boy's hand. "I need you to hold this here on your mother's wound. Keep applying pressure until I return."

"What if…what if you don't come back?" the boy asked.

Captain Action smiled so confidently that the youth found he was grinning in return. "I *will* be back. Now be a hero like El Terror Negro."

"No," the boy said, shaking his head. "Like Captain Action!"

■ ■ ■

Rex was laughing, the maniacal sound mixing with the deadly melody of gunfire and screaming. He held a rifle in his right hand and an automatic pistol in his left, both weapons spewing death with unerring accuracy. He killed indiscriminately, not caring the age or gender of his victims. In fact, he almost seemed to relish killing the innocent for several times he avoided shooting warriors to pick off an old man or young woman that was running about for safety.

In many ways, he was the perfect mercenary. For the right price, he was prepared to do almost anything with no questions asked. His skills, combined with a lack of morals, had put him in high demand. If there was a war going on anywhere in the world, he'd had a part to play in it—often, he'd fought on both sides of the same conflict.

He loved the money and spent it freely…but he would have killed and fought for free, if he'd had to. Thankfully, he'd been saved from that by his old mentor, Jack Oat—the man had recognized something in Rex and had taken him in after he'd been drummed out of the military for being a bit too zealous in some regards. Jack had honed his abilities and taught him the techniques that only the CIA's best possessed.

Then, when he'd learned all that he could, Rex had cut the ties that bound him to Oat. He'd struck out on his own, carving out a reputation as the hot new thing in the world of guns for hire. It hadn't always been glamorous but it had never failed to be interesting.

Rex barely heard the pound of footsteps over the din of battle. He turned his head at the last second and spotted The Gibbon sprinting towards him. The masked jungle lord launched himself into the air, striking with both feet against Rex's left side. The impact was enough to knock the mercenary back several feet but he retained his balance and didn't fall to the ground.

Tossing aside his rifle, Rex reached up and snatched off the full facemask that he'd been wearing. His face glistened with sweat and his eyes were wide, full of madness. "I showed you mine," he taunted. "Now—show me yours."

The Gibbon seemed in no mood for games. He extended his right hand quickly, his entire weight behind the punch he was throwing. Rex ducked down and knocked the other man's arm aside before delivering his own physical retort—a rabbit punch that caught The Gibbon in the throat. The bigger man gasped for air and Rex pushed the advantage by backhanding his opponent with the butt of his pistol. Blood flew from The Gibbon's mouth as his lip tore.

"I've heard about you," Rex said, allowing The Gibbon a moment to recover. Though death was continuing to fall all around them, both men's attention had become extremely focused. All else was a blur—only each other were in sharp relief. "They say you're a walking dead man, a ghost. They say you'll live as long as the jungle does."

"That's truth," The Gibbon replied, turning his steely gaze upon Rex. "Men may die, but ideas can live forever."

"That sounds pretty stupid." Rex spun about, a leg kick aimed at The Gibbon's head. The lord of the jungle avoided it with ease but Rex was on the attack again as soon as both feet were back on the ground. He struck with a flurry of punches, most of which The Gibbon was able to block—but a few got past the bigger man's defenses, landing hard against his ribs.

To an outsider, the rapid blows were almost impossible to follow—but to trained fighters, certain aspects of style began to creep in. The movements and responses of both The Gibbon and Rex began to display similarities... and this was not lost on the combatants.

Rex grunted as The Gibbon struck him down in the chin, causing him to accidentally bite down on his tongue. He spat out a mouthful of blood, some of it dripping down his face. "It's you, isn't it, Jack? This is what the old man's been reduced to? Playing dress-up in the jungle?"

"Scoff if you want, but I've found my purpose in life."

Rex cackled in disbelief. "These jungle girls must have ruined your mind, Jack. I get it that you'd enjoy playing king but you're in the middle of nowhere! I tell you what—come with me. If you toe the line and do what

I say, I'll make you my right-hand man. What do you say?"

The Gibbon's response came in the form of a physical assault—he led with a right hand before following it up with a left hook that would have taken Rex's block off. Unfortunately, Rex was the faster of the two. He avoided the second punch and instead drove the barrel of gun up under the big man's outstretched arm, pushing it hard against Jack's chest. He pulled the trigger and a single bullet ripped through animal skin, cloth, skin and bone before passing through Jack's heart.

Jack staggered back, a look of shock evident on his face. Both hands came up to clutch his chest and he fell to his knees, blood beginning to bubble up from between his tightly clenched lips. His throat began to make a gurgling sound and Rex extended the toe of a boot to push his old mentor over onto his back.

"Guess that whole bit about ideas never dying didn't really work out for you, huh?" Rex taunted. Spinning on his heels, the mercenary leader turned away and took aim once more. He pulled the trigger, killing a native warrior that was running by, and then began shouting orders for his men to pull back. The fight was over, The Gibbon's surviving forces scattered. The last remaining threat to Dr. Evil's scheme had been removed and Rex anticipated a healthy reward upon his return.

■ ■ ■

Captain Action fired his pistol, unloading the last of its charges. The lightning-like burst took out his opponent, a somewhat stocky mercenary armed with a bayonet.

Panting, The Captain whirled about to continue the fight but he noticed that the mercenaries were now leaving the scene en masse. A quick glance around the camp told him why: the place was a mess, with some huts ablaze and bodies lying everywhere.

Captain Action spotted a familiar form in the center of the camp and he raced forward, kneeling at the side of The Gibbon. The jungle lord was still alive, though barely.

"Hang in there, Jack."

"Too…late," came the gurgled reply. The Gibbon seized Captain Action's hand and squeezed it hard. "Mustn't let them…win. Please."

Captain Action frowned but he nodded. He looked about and saw that no one was watching them. Everyone seemed to be either in shock or lost in their own private troubles. He reached under the fallen jungle lord and lifted him up, straining due to Jack's tremendous size. "Don't worry, Jack…I'll do everything I can to protect these people."

"I fear he may no longer be able to hear you, Captain."

Drake turned his head and saw that his earlier sense that no one had seen them had been been wrong. Kawil gestured towards the cave and Captain Action hurriedly began moving in that direction. "I'm sorry, Kawil."

"As am I. We are not without hope, however. Twice before in my lifetime I have seen The Gibbon fall in battle—and twice before has he returned to us!"

Captain Action ducked into the darkness of the cave, relieved when the torches bloomed to life. "Kawil…tell no one of this. It would only cause pointless fear."

"Agreed." Kawil started to leave, stopping only when Captain Action asked where he was going. "Your woman—Selena, I believe? She is here in the camp. I will bring her to you."

"Do that—but first: I left a little boy out there with his injured mother. He was the El Terror Negro fan that you saw me speaking to earlier. Make sure he and his mom are taken care of."

"I give you my word," Kawil said.

Drake nodded, waiting until he was alone to lift away The Gibbon's mask. He saw the face of Jack Oat, as he knew he would. The man was dead and with him went many secrets.

SEVENTEEN: GHOSTLY RETURN

Selena was staring daggers at Kawil from the moment he came to untie her. Her foul mood didn't improve as he led her through the ruined mess of the camp—so many dead, with large numbers of old and young mixed in among the warriors.

"I could have helped," she said.

Kawil did not reply but she saw his jaw clench as he bit back some sort of retort. He had only said one thing since he came to free her: "Selena, I am sorry. I will now take you to your friend."

True to his word, he took her into The Gibbon's cave, where she was relieved to see Captain Action. The Directorate operative was sitting wearily in The Gibbon's throne, the dead body of the jungle lord on the floor at his feet. The domino-style mask that had partially hid the man's features now lay across The Gibbon's chest. His true identity of Jack Oat was now revealed, though Selena was already aware of it. From the lack of surprise on Kawil's face, he also knew of the deception.

As if sensing her deduction, Kawil said, "The spirit of The Gibbon is such that it was able to enter Jack Oat's heart and transform him. Once he put on the furs, he was no longer an agent of your CIA…he recognized the importance of something greater: the protection of a sacred land and its people."

Selena rolled her eyes and muttered, "*Estas loco.*"

Captain Action stood up at that moment. He wasn't smiling—the strains of battle and the deaths he had witnessed were too much for that— but Selena could see in his eyes that he was glad to see her. "Selena—I was worried about you."

She stepped quickly towards him and both of them started to open their arms for an embrace. They hesitated and the moment passed somewhat awkwardly. Seeking to move past the strange silence that fell between them, Selena said, "Jack followed me when we split up before. He was angry that I was going to bring back more help and so he knocked me out. When I came to, I was gagged and tied up. When the fighting started, I was convinced that I was going to die like that."

"It was Rex's men."

"That's what I assumed—did you find out anything else?"

"Dr. Evil is definitely behind it all and they're trying to dig up some sort of large meteor that crashed here a long time ago."

Selena put her hands on her hips. "Then we definitely need to call in some backup! Who knows what that madman's up to?"

"Not to revive our earlier disagreement but I think we have to move faster than that—even though Rex and I didn't run into each other during the battle, I'm sure some of his people will report having seen me. When that gets back to Dr. Evil, he might decide to bolt. We need to rally any surviving fighters we have here and head to Evil's camp."

This time, Selena didn't argue that point. She agreed that they couldn't afford to let Evil get away. "My only concern is that these people were just torn apart by Rex's men. Their friends and families are dead or injured. They're not going to want to follow us into battle."

"They would if The Gibbon told them to," Kawil said.

Selena looked at him in confusion. "Are you going to lie to them and say he gave them orders to go back into the fight?"

"No," Drake said. "He's saying that The Gibbon needs to live again."

Selena's eyes roved over Kawil's body and she shrugged. "You're not built anything like Jack and you don't have a beard…but maybe you can pull it off."

Kawil straightened up and shook his head. "I would never do such a thing. I am a priest—I fight, yes, but my purpose is to counsel The Gibbon. I am not fit to wear the sacred vestments."

"Then who—?" Selena's eyes widened. "Miles…?"

Captain Action removed his cap and set it down in the throne. He began to remove his uniform, as well, stripping down to a pair of tight-fitting briefs. If he was embarrassed to be in front of Selena in his underwear, he didn't show it—though she blushed quite noticeably. It was a bit of a turnaround from what had happened when they first met, when he'd asked her to turn her back while he changed. She wondered what it meant that he was more comfortable in her presence now…while she was more embarrassed. It was strange.

Miles was taking out a handful of plastiderm from the pouches of his suit. Selena had never seen its like before—it resembled some sort of clay but it seemed to shift in his grip, almost like it was alive. "This material is called plastiderm," Miles said. "It allows me to alter my appearance so that I can pass for almost anyone on the planet. With a bit of help from my makeup kit and my own skill at mimicking people, I think I can fool everyone into thinking that I'm The Gibbon—at least the Jack Oat variety." He looked at Kawil. "While I'm applying this, can you remove The Gibbon uniform from Jack?"

"I'll do it," Selena piped up. "I get the feeling that Kawil would prefer not to handle the 'sacred' garments. Right?"

Kawil nodded somewhat gratefully. "You are wise beyond your years, Lady of Action."

Selena smirked at Miles. "I'm telling you—if I wasn't already La Marsopa, there's a perfectly good codename there for the taking."

■ ■ ■

The process took less than fifteen minutes and when it was done, Selena was positive that not even someone that had known Jack Oat as The Gibbon for years would have noticed the difference. It was uncanny how effective the disguise truly was—not only in just the way that Drake's face had been transformed but in the way that he stood, the slight cock of his head and the firm, steely gaze that he now possessed. It was as if Miles Drake had been swallowed up by the ghost of The Gibbon.

"You feel it, don't you?" Kawil asked. "The weight of responsibility and the power of the furs?"

The Gibbon looked at Kawil and nodded gravely. "I do feel it but not for the reasons you presume. I know that the men and women outside this cave need something to believe in and that they'd do virtually anything I asked, at least as long as I look like this. I don't want to betray that trust, Kawil. So, yes, I can see how Jack or any man worth his salt could be taken in by the experience of becoming The Gibbon."

Kawil seemed satisfied by the response. "I will go out and gather our warriors. I will tell them that The Gibbon will address them soon."

When the priest was gone, Selena ran a hand through her hair and sighed. "Miles, do you think this is fair to them?"

"What do you mean?"

"They're exhausted and most of them just saw friends and family massacred in front of them. Now we're talking about dragging them off into another firefight that they're going to outmatched in."

"If you were one of them and your family and friends had just been killed or hurt, wouldn't you want to strike back at your enemy?"

Selena's expression clouded over and for a moment, Miles felt like he'd stepped over some sort of line. She looked like she was thinking back to something specific, perhaps another place and another time. "If someone had done this to my family, Miles, I would kill them all," she said in a low voice.

"Selena…"

She looked up and whatever dark feeling had taken hold of her was gone. Once again he saw that playful light in her eyes. "You win, Miles—and I have to say, you look good in that outfit. There's just one thing, though…."

"What's that?"

"That gibbon fur needs to be washed out every now and then. It stinks to high heaven!"

■ ■ ■

Captain Action stared out at the hardened faces assembled before him. In all, there were only about three dozen warriors left and many of them had been injured to some degree during the battle. They looked resolute and eager to gain revenge on the mercenaries that had invaded their homes.

With Kawil and Selena standing just behind him, Captain Action began to pace back and forth in front of the warriors. He moved like a jungle cat, remembering the detailed description that Kawil had given him of The Gibbon's usual means of addressing his people. When he spoke, his voice was indistinguishable from the one that Jack Oat had used. "The men who attacked us serve one whose heart is black as night! In the so-called world of 'civilized' men he is called Evil...Dr. Evil. He is here to rape our land and use its secrets for his own dark purpose. He cares nothing for the trees, for the animals or for us. He will burn this jungle to the ground if it serves his vile schemes. The only way to protect our land and our people is to stop him...and now I ask you to rise up one more time. If you are willing to follow me, I will lead you into battle and into victory." 'The Gibbon' stopped in place and he looked into the eyes of each and every man, holding their gaze for a few seconds before moving on to the next. When he had taken the measure of every man, he nodded and said, "I know what I ask of you. When I fall in battle, I rise again. When you fall, your spirit leaves this place. It is not as hard for me to risk my life when I know that I shall not truly die...that is why I want every one of you to know that the real hero is not The Gibbon. It is each and every one of my warriors, who give their all for their wives, for their children...and for me."

Kawil stepped forward then and raised both hands. "Who shall follow The Gibbon?" he bellowed.

In unison, the warriors raised their right hands and punched the sky with clenched fists. Their voices cried out with every punch, imitating the cry of the jungle lord.

Captain Action didn't try to stop the smile from spreading across his face. He threw his head back and performed The Gibbon's cry, the inhuman sound echoing for many miles around.

■ ■ ■

Rex lit a cigar and ran his fingers through the hair of the frightened young woman that he'd claimed as his prize during the attack on The Gibbon's lair. It was his habit to let his men take a few women as rewards for their hard work and he'd indulged his own hateful lusts this time. If killing your mentor wasn't reason enough for celebration, what was?

He didn't feel any regret over what had happened to Jack. The man had always been an odd one—Rex remembered in the early days of their partnership, when Jack would sometimes talk at length about stepping 'outside the law' in order to bring justice to those that needed it. The old man had actually thought that being a mercenary could be something noble. Rex had thought it crazy at the time—but that was nothing compared to actually dressing up like a monkey and living in the jungle. What the hell had Jack been thinking?

The woman that served as Rex's prize was somewhere between sixteen years of age and twenty—Rex found it hard to tell with some of these girls. She flinched at his touch and he leaned close to her, blowing smoke into her face. "Can you understand English, doll?" She stared at him blankly, her eyes wide with fear. "Of course you don't. I didn't pick you because you looked smart."

Rex laughed as he lowered his hand from her hair and copped a feel. She looked like she wanted to knock his hand away but she knew better. It didn't usually take much to impress upon people that Rex wasn't to be trifled with. There was something in his eyes that made it clear that he was capable of being cruel.

A knock at the door made Rex frown. He turned away from the girl, who drew up her legs and wrapped her arms tightly about them. She was sitting on Rex's bed, backed up as far against the wall as possible.

"What is it?" he demanded. He set his cigar down in an ashtray.

The voice of Montgomery, his second-in-command, answered. "We have a problem."

"You're going to have a problem if this turns out to be unimportant—I was getting ready to learn more about my new friend." Rex strode over to the door and yanked it open. Montgomery had a slightly weasel-like look to him and he craned his neck to see past Rex, hoping to see some skin from the local girl. When he saw she was still fully dressed, the disappointment was obvious. "Well?" Rex prompted.

"You know how we posted scouts all around the camp?"

Rex slapped Montgomery on the side of the head. "Yeah, it was my orders to do it! Get to the point."

Montgomery looked angry but he felt too cowed by Rex to respond to the physical blow in kind. "None of them have reported in—I sent out a couple of guys to check on them and they didn't come back either."

Rex looked confused. He stroked his chin. "What the hell—? It can't be

The Gibbon's people. We left them picking themselves up off the ground in pieces."

"We heard the cry, too."

Rex grabbed hold of Montgomery's shirt and yanked him close. "Don't play games with me. The Gibbon is dead…it was Jack Oat in that stinking outfit and I killed him myself. Are you sure you didn't just hear an actual gibbon and now you're showing how yellow you are?"

"I know what I heard, Rex."

"Fine." He shoved Montgomery away. "Go and round up some of the boys. I'll lead them out into the woods."

"Should I tell Dr. Evil?"

"No. He hired us to handle things like this and that's what we're going to do. I'll be out in about five minutes."

Montgomery nodded and hurried away. Rex shut the door and started speaking even before he'd turned back to the girl. "I'm afraid our little party's going to have to wait, sweetcakes."

The girl was right in front of him, slamming the lit end of the cigar into his face. It burned the side of his right cheek, just below his eye. He howled in pain and backhanded her so hard that she flew away from him and dropped the cigar. Her head struck the edge of the bedframe as she fell to the floor and she landed hard on her back.

Rex ignored her for a moment, hurrying over to the washbasin. He splashed water on his wound and then looked into the mirror he used for shaving. It looked pretty nasty and he was certain it was going to leave a scar.

Roaring, he turned and delivered a powerful kick into the prone woman's side. She was still breathing but she was out cold.

Rex strapped on his gun belt and stormed out of the room. There was a chance she might die without medical attention but that was her own fault—if she'd played nice, nobody would have gotten hurt. Assuming she was still alive when he came back, she'd learn the full depth of her mistake.

He howled in pain and backhanded her...

EIGHTEEN: CLOUDED MIND

The attack came suddenly and without warning.

From various points above, bullets and rocks were propelled down into the mining camp. Many workers and guards were felled before they even knew they were in danger, victims of the unerring accuracy of The Gibbon's people. The locals may have been outnumbered and outgunned but they had one thing that could potentially change the outcome: these were people fighting not just for their lives but for their very homes.

After the initial airborne assault, a party of warriors burst into the enemy's midst, carrying the fight to them on a hand-to-hand level. With this group were Selena, Kawil and Captain Action disguised as The Gibbon. The Captain maintained his ruse even in battle, fighting with the style that had been described to him—much like the animal whose skin and name he had adopted, The Gibbon fought with a terrifying ferocity, barking and growling all the time. He favored brute strength but was not above acrobatic displays in combat. As such, Captain Action howled as he descended upon his surprised enemies, lowering his shoulder and barreling right through some of them before leaping atop a parked jeep and springing off at a miner that was trying to run to safety. He knocked this man out and moved on, hoping that the rest of his forces would remember his orders: non-lethal attacks on the workers, whatever it took on the mercenaries.

The Gibbon would spare those that were relatively innocent laborers… but for Rex's men, there was only the harsh justice of the jungle.

■ ■ ■

Selena was armed with a knife, preferring to keep her sidearm holstered for now. She grinned like a madwoman as she cut a swath through Rex's men. They were well-trained and beginning to formulate an organized response but the many people that were here for menial labor worked against them. The non-combatants were running about in terror, many of them getting in the way of those that were trying to defend the camp.

These were moments when Selena felt most confident. No matter how hard she tried, she was always held back in the eyes of others by her gender, as if the fact that she was a woman somehow made her less worthy of respect than her male counterparts. She had to do three times the work of the men in her division in order to attain the same level of authority—and then she'd had to do even more to become Mexico's top agent. It was a precarious honor, even then—one screw-up and it would be blamed on her gender, forcing her back to handling small-scale operations.

In battle, there was no time for anyone to focus on anything other than her skill, her ferocity and her blade. Selena knew that Miles was similar in this respect—she'd recognized it in his eyes when they'd fought side-by-side earlier. He was, as his codename suggested, someone that preferred action to inactivity. It was one of the many things that made him attractive to her. Working with nearly all males had caused her to adopt many traditionally masculine personality traits, however—one of which was that she was uncomfortable expressing emotion for fear that it would somehow be used against her. She hid her feelings behind a mask of sarcastic humor, always allowing herself the 'out' that maybe her admiration was meant in jest. Thus, her constant teasing of Miles Drake, a man that she felt a strong desire for. Of course, in the end it didn't matter. In their line of work, there was little room for romance—even if they slept with one another and pledged fealty, they would be sent to different parts of the world by their respective masters and might even be called upon to spy on each other.

And, of course, there was the fact that Miles was obviously still hung up on his ex.

All of these thoughts were running through her mind as she fought her way towards the center of camp—she and Miles were not only trying to defeat the enemy but they had other goals, as well: locating Uliana and her Russian companion while also capturing Dr. Evil. Her eyes swept across the camp, trying to find any sign of Evil or his prisoners. She did spot something interesting, though it wasn't what she was hoping for. Rex, the man that had killed Jack Oat, was striding towards her, a grin on his unmasked face. A nasty-looking burn on that face caught her eye and she assumed that there was quite a story behind that.

"La Marsopa," he called out. "Why am I not surprised to see you? You and your boyfriend must be too stupid to realize when you're outclassed."

Selena sneered in reply, "That's funny coming from you, Señor. You're nothing more than a preening fool. You win these battles because of all your hombres that you bring with you, not from skill."

Rex's expression darkened. "I killed Jack Oat—while he was wearing that 'sacred' gibbon skin. I'd say that's pretty impressive, wouldn't you?"

"You killed an old man dressed in stinky furs. I'm not impressed."

Rex unsheathed a long knife that had been strapped to his leg. "If you're asking for me to try and impress you, chica—I'm willing to do it."

Selena felt a sense of accomplishment when Rex came for her—if he'd maintained his composure, he could have picked her off easily with one of the many guns that were strapped to his sides or slung over his back. Instead, he'd allowed her to challenge his masculine pride and now he was foolishly coming in for melee combat.

Rex struck first, stabbing at Selena's hip with his knife. She parried the attack with ease and the two began exchanging a series of moves designed to test the defenses of the other. Neither was found wanting as each was able to avoid the blows and smoothly follow up with an attack of their own.

Selena allowed the clamor of the surrounding battle to fade away—in her heightened sense of awareness, there was nothing but her and Rex. She noticed the way sweat beaded on the end of his nose before falling to the ground and the way he blinked his eyes hard at the end of every stabbing attempt that he made. He was good but he wasn't flawless—he visibly allowed his emotions to affect his fighting style, for both good and ill.

"Have you ever lost a fight to a girl before, Rex?" she teased, swiping the edge of her blade near her opponent's throat. The move was an unexpected switch from her previous attacks, which had mainly been focused on his torso. She caught his skin, drawing first blood, even if it was only a thin red line. "I mean, I'm sure you've disappointed plenty but I mean a total failure," she added.

Rex growled in the back of his throat. "I'm going to make you scream."

"This is probably the only way you could, pelele."

Rex apparently recognized the Spanish word for 'wimp' because he increased the ferocity of his attacks, repeatedly stabbing at her in a frenzy of motion. Selena avoided most of the strikes but one of them caught her in the left shoulder—it was mostly a flesh wound but it still hurt like hell and caused her to cry out.

"That's just foreplay, doll," Rex taunted. He looked inordinately pleased with himself and for a moment his defenses fell—he was celebrating the small victory and obviously expected her to fold now that she had experienced pain.

That was his fatal mistake.

Selena spun about, generating extra force behind her attack. Her blade once again was aimed towards his throat—this time his lack of preparation led to something worse than a small cut. Her sharpened blade dug deep into his skin and struck his esophagus. She felt her knife tear through skin and tissue as it ripped its way out on the other side of his neck. Blood sprayed from the wound in a shocking display before shifting into a steady pulse of red fluid gushing out over the hands that he rose to staunch the flow.

His eyes were wide now and he opened his mouth like a fish—no words came out, only a strange gurgling sound that was like music to Selena's ears.

Rex, the man that had styled himself a slayer of legends, fell over backward. He landed in a twitching heap and Selena contemplated letting him suffer as he bled out—but she was not the monster that he was. She raised her knife and brought the weapon down for a killing blow, burying the blade deep in his heart. She gave it a twist and then yanked it free, already turning her attention to the war going on around her. There would be time for relishing her triumph later—for now, she had more enemies to slay.

■ ■ ■

Captain Action was a whirling dervish of activity—as The Gibbon, he painted a flamboyant figure and that attracted many of the enemy. While at first he was busy dodging bullets, it proved inevitable that many of the mercenaries wanted to be able to personally take credit for slaying the leader of their enemy. As such, he quickly found himself surrounded by men armed with clubs and edged weapons.

A master of many forms of combat, Captain Action slipped from one style to the next with ease. One moment he was using judo to toss a burly opponent over his shoulder, the next he was adopting traditional boxing methods to deliver a roundhouse punch that knocked one man out cold.

A machete whistled past his head, a killing blow that was narrowly avoided by the Captain's instincts. He seized hold of the man's wrist and twisted it expertly—the cracking of bones was almost overwhelmed by the man's scream of pain. The machete slipped from the mercenary's grip and Captain Action plucked it right out of the air. He would have preferred to use his own unique weapons but for now it was part of the game to pretend to be The Gibbon—and the jungle lord's usage of Captain Action's arsenal might have brought questions from the faithful.

The machete proved to be a suitable replacement and two of the mercenaries were felled by deep cuts that left them writhing on the ground. It was challenging to use a bladed weapon to incapacitate an enemy without killing them but Captain Action was well versed in the anatomy of the human body—he knew without thinking where he could strike and how deeply he could stab without causing a fatal injury.

Through the din, Captain Action heard something that froze the blood in his veins. A woman's scream, abruptly cut off—and it belonged to a woman whose voice he knew as well as his own. "Uliana," he whispered.

He turned towards the sound of the scream, dispatching a mercenary with a backhanded blow that knocked him flat. He spotted the building where he'd seen Dr. Stefan Tracy earlier and he realized that the woman had to be inside there. He sprinted that way, dodging attacks and leaping over fallen bodies.

The door to the building was closed so he lowered his shoulder and rammed it with all the force he could muster. Just like the Cleveland Browns' star running back Leroy Kelly, he hammered his way forward, refusing to yield until he'd fought his way through to the other side.

The hut consisted of one main room with two smaller ones attached. Against the far wall he saw Uliana and Juthrbog, restrained by thick ropes. Both of them wore tattered clothing and had bruises on their faces and upper bodies. Uliana also had a set of strange tubes attached to her waist—they looked much like the devices that Drake had seen stuck into the ground outside during his first visit to the camp. Every time the devices glowed with light, Uliana seemed to wither somewhat, as if her very lifeforce was being drained right out of her.

The thought of Uliana being tortured made him see red—and that accounted for his lack of awareness.

"Miles!" Uliana screamed. "Behind you!"

He started to turn but it was too late—something heavy slammed into the back of his head and the room suddenly began to swim. Captain Action spun about and landed on his back. As darkness began to close in around him, he saw the face that often haunted his nightmares: a blue-skinned humanoid with cat-like yellow eyes. The top of his attacker's skull appeared to be missing, exposing an oversized brain—in truth, Captain Action knew that the man's skull was simply so transparent that it appeared invisible. Tiny flashes of electricity could be seen in the brain tissue, flashing with every burst of cerebral processing.

This was Dr. Evil, the single greatest threat to humanity.

"Hello, Captain," Dr. Evil purred triumphantly.

And then Miles Drake heard no more.

NINETEEN: PRIME ENERGY

Cold water splashed into Captain Action's face, awakening him with a start. He jerked forward but found his arms and legs were restrained by chains, binding him to heavy oak table in one of the rooms of Evil's abode. He could hear Uliana and Juthrbog's voices in the adjoining area, whispering words of concern to one another. While he badly wanted to see his love again, his focus was drawn to the source of the water that had reawakened him: Dr. Evil.

The brilliant but corrupt scientist stood in front of him, an empty bucket held in one hand. The villain was smiling, the electrical sparks around his brain looking faster than usual. "We meet again, Captain. I have to say, as atrocious as your usual garb is, I prefer it to the animal skins."

"You're one to talk," Miles muttered. Dr. Evil was still dressed in the garb of Stefan Tracy, so the hippie attire looked even more out of place when coupled with the alien-like facial features.

Ignoring the jibe, Evil cocked his head to the side and asked, "Do you hear that?"

Captain Action paused, for a moment confused by what he meant. Then the significance began to sink in: he heard silence. The battle was over.

"Your people put up a good fight, Captain, but they have pulled back. We can still see them but they're obviously not sure if they should continue on with their suicidal effort or turn tail and run. I wonder," he tapped his chin thoughtfully. "Do you think they're waiting for a signal from The Gibbon? That's who they think you are, am I right? Well, except for that splendid specimen of femininity that the Mexican government paired you with. You have remarkable luck in that regard, Captain. You always end up with the loveliest of partners."

"What are you up to, Tracy? Why are you hiding out in the jungle, digging for rocks?"

Dr. Evil flinched when Drake referred him to by his old name. When his real face was on display, the villain was touchy about being reminded of the past. "The 'rocks' as you say aren't important, Captain—it's what they contain that's essential. Speaking of which, I have to thank you for helping deliver the New Lake woman into my hands. Turns out that she's the final piece of the puzzle for my plan to succeed."

Knowing that Tracy's fatal flaw was his ego, Captain Action decided to play to that. He sagged in his bonds, looking defeated. "It's too late, isn't it?" he asked. "You've completed your work here."

"More or less, yes. A few little details are left to take care of but ultimately, I've accomplished all that I needed to. The Alchemy is complete."

"You're turning things into gold?"

"Now you are simply being inane," Evil gloated. "No, my Alchemy is of a different kind. As you know, I've been somewhat obsessed in recent years with the acquisition of Prime Energies—you successfully ruined my attempts to harness them from the rocks in New Lake and Japan, but my defeats there actually served a useful purpose because they led me to discover the mother lode of Prime Energies—the radioactive power of the meteor that ended the reign of the dinosaurs! That's right, Captain, right now you and I are standing atop the largest chunk of that meteor—and I've spent the past few months draining the Prime Energies from every piece I could find! I was still somewhat short of the amount I needed... and then Uliana dropped into my lap again. It turns out that I can drain Prime Energies directly from human beings, if their bodies have absorbed enough of it in the past."

"To what purpose?"

Dr. Evil melodramatically looked skyward and cackled. He turned away and said, "I'm not *that* stupid, Captain. I love a good monologue as much as anyone, but I'm not going to 'spill all the beans' about my plans... After all, I've learned again and again that until you are dead, you are still a potential threat."

"So why didn't you kill me while you had the chance?" Captain Action asked. This part wasn't just part of his plan to gather information...he was legitimately curious.

"I should have," Dr. Evil said, nodding to himself. He was walking out of the room but he paused in the doorway. His eyes locked onto Captain Action's and he admitted, "I have no equals in this world, Captain—and neither do you. In a strange way, you and I are all the other really has. At the moment of my triumph, I wanted you to be there. I wanted you to see and to know."

Captain Action had no response to that—to be honest, it was the answer that he would have expected. This strange relationship between the two men had grown past simple rivalry. There was an odd sort of respect there, intermingled with all the hate. If and when Captain Action died, he almost felt like it had to be in pitched battle with the former Stefan Tracy. Anything less would have seemed inappropriate for the both of them.

"Strip him—but be gentle with the outfit. I'm going to need it," Dr. Evil said, exiting the room. On cue, two burly men entered, one of them brandishing scissors and the other sporting a rather nasty grin.

"Uh, guys, I wouldn't do that if I were you," Captain Action muttered.

"Why's that?" the man with the grin asked.

"Because this animal skin is sacred. If you cause any damage to it, you're going to pay."

"We'll take that risk."

■ ■ ■

When the process was done, Miles Drake no longer resembled The Gibbon. The men had removed the jungle lord's garments from him and even peeled away the plastiderm disguise. Underneath the furs he'd worn his Captain Action uniform, his weapons and cap strapped to his belt. He was glad he hadn't elected to go with just his skivvies under the suit.

The men had done their job with a fair amount of professionalism, carefully slicing off the garments in a way that they weren't ruined. The one with the sickly smile had 'accidentally' nicked the Captain's flesh a few times with his knife and had been quite disappointed that the pricks had elicited nothing more than the occasional flinch from his captive. Captain Action had refused to give the sicko any pleasure and had refrained from emitting any noises of pain.

Once he was alone, however, Captain Action allowed his body to sag and the weariness that he felt to momentarily take over. He tried not to think about the odds facing him but it was hard not to. Even if he managed to get free of this, how would he manage to get Uliana to safety? How was he going to stop Dr. Evil's latest scheme?

Give it a rest, he told himself. *Take things one step at a time.*

It was still quiet outside but surely Selena would encourage their forces to strike again soon. If Miles was going to help in any way, he needed to get free.

Closing his eyes and steeling himself for the coming pain, he began to rotate his left arm in a circular motion. The chains rattled a bit as he moved but not too loudly—and then he suddenly gave a twist. He grunted between clenched teeth, having just popped his shoulder out of the socket. His arm hung at a slightly strange angle now and through the haze of pain he was able to slide it forward now in a way that he couldn't before. The new position allowed him to place the chains between his feet and he applied his full weight upon them. The pressure on his wrists was intense but this was far from his first rodeo — he knew exactly how far he could push his body without breaking bones.

The chains began to give under his strength and one of the links suddenly popped, allowing his right arm to come free. Now it was a relatively simple matter of taking a pick from his belt and undoing the locks.

Less than five minutes after he'd begun his escape attempt, Captain Action was free. He snapped his arm back into its socket and then took a moment to let the pain subside. It still ached terribly but it was functional and that was all that mattered.

Footsteps in the hall caused him to move quickly. He sprang to his feet, pulling free his lighting sword and holding it at the ready as he took up a position just inside the door, out of sight of whoever was coming. With luck it would be Dr. Evil, returning to gloat some more—if that was the case, then this whole awful affair could be put to bed quickly.

The figure that entered the room was not Dr. Evil, however. It was the goon with the unhealthy interest in making Miles bleed. The Captain struck quickly, grabbing the man from behind and placing the edge of his blade against his throat. "Keep your voice down," he warned, "or I'll silence you forever."

The man tried to swallow but he found the edge of the blade made that difficult. "Dr. Evil's gone," the man hissed. "He finished with your woman and then left."

Captain Action felt his heart skip a beat but he forced himself to keep his mind on the mission. "Where did he go? Is he leaving the camp?"

"Not just yet...there's still the matter of loading all the stolen Prime Energy onto the trucks. Until then, he needs to keep the natives from attacking. So he's gone to speak to them as The Gibbon."

Now it made sense—that was why he'd wanted The Gibbon's garments.

Captain Action drew his blade away from the man before slamming the hilt of it down on the back of the mercenary's skull.

After trussing the man up in the chains and shoving a dirty rag into his mouth to keep him quiet if he woke up, Captain Action re-entered the main room of the hut. He found himself shaking somewhat, afraid of what he might find. Dr. Evil had 'finished' with Uliana…did that mean she was dead?

Uliana and Juthrbog were still where he had last seen them, tied to the wall…but Uliana sagged like a broken doll, her eyes closed and her chest barely moving.

"Oh, no," Captain Action whispered.

"She is dying," Juthrbog said, his expression even more grim than usual. "And it is all your fault!"

TWENTY: LISTEN TO YOUR HEART

Selena stared down at the campsite, her fists clenched at her sides. In the minutes since she had reluctantly pulled back their forces, the mercenaries had assumed defensive positions while the workers set about pulling up the transparent tubes that were placed into the earth. These tubes, glowing with some strange power, were now being loaded onto a large truck.

"Where are you, Miles?" she asked.

"The Gibbon can never die."

Selena glanced to see Kawil standing beside her. The priest had dried blood on his chest and chin—some of it his own, most belonging to others. "I'm surprised to hear you say that," she said. "We both saw Jack Oat's dead body, after all."

"Jack Oat was just a vessel for the legend. Whenever The Gibbon dies, another arises to take his place. It has always been this way—and I believe it shall be this way for many years to come."

Selena looked back at the injured and exhausted men that were waiting for whatever was to come next. They were not broken, despite the fact that they had suffered several losses in rapid succession. They still seemed to believe…just as Kawil did. "How can you maintain this faith of yours, when you know it's all falsification?"

"It is *not* fake! Stop thinking with your civilized mind and start listening with your heart! I can sense that you want to be a part of something greater than yourself and that same feeling is what binds all of my people together."

"I'm sorry, Kawil. It just…it all seems so strange to me. Being a part of the government's espionage program, I hunt down enemies of the state. I look for clues and facts. I make decisions that are based upon my observations and my deductions."

"But in battle, you can't always do that," Kawil countered. "You must make choices that are sometimes based upon a hunch or intuition. Maintaining faith in The Gibbon is more like that than anything else. You feel that it is right to offer up your life to protect your people and your land…and you do it. You trust that the man in the mystic furs will lead us to victory."

"But what if the man in the furs isn't up to the task?"

"Jack Oat became something greater than himself as The Gibbon…and the Man of Action will do the same. The man that was The Gibbon before Jack was a wonderful man. He taught me much about myself and about life…when he died, I had my doubts about Jack but it didn't take long for me to realize that he was no longer the man he had been before. He started out playing The Gibbon, mimicking the actions of his predecessor, but soon he *was* the role he had been playing."

"Fake it 'til you make it," Selena whispered with a smile.

"What is that?" Kawil asked.

"Just something I heard once—a friend of mine went through a program called Alcoholics Anonymous. Have you heard of it?"

"No."

"Well, the phrase basically means that you go through the motions of something as if it were real…until eventually it becomes real."

"A wise saying."

"Kawil! He comes!"

Kawil and Selena looked over at a man who was pointing down the hill. Following his gaze, they saw The Gibbon ascending the cliff, hauling himself up to face them. There was no doubt that these were the mystic furs...but both of them immediately doubted that this was Miles Drake. Whoever this was, they were skilled in mimicry but there was a flaw in their performance: there was none of the warmth that they had come to recognize as part of Miles Drake's essence.

■ ■ ■

"My people!" The Gibbon shouted. Everyone rose and came forward to listen to him. "We have won this day—our enemies are making preparations to leave this place and never return!"

An exultant cry broke out amongst the warriors—the only ones not joining in were Selena and Kawil, both of whom watched in silence.

The Gibbon motioned for silence and his men responded by eagerly leaning forward to hear what came next. "Lay down your arms and return home—I shall remain here to make sure that they abide by our terms. But know this: it was through your bravery, your blood and your sweat, that we have triumphed!"

There was a murmur of surprise that rippled through the troops. They had obviously not expected this turn of events. Why were they not driving the defeated from their lands? Were they really going back home and trusting the outsiders to live up to their promises?

The Gibbon continued, "I know it is strange, my people...but I will personally remain behind to oversee the departure of our enemies. When they are gone, we will finally be safe."

Several warriors began to turn about but Kawil stopped them by shouting, "This is a lie!"

Gasps and murmurings from the assembled warriors almost brought a smile to Selena's face. All of them knew that Kawil was a devout follower of The Gibbon—and she was fairly certain that none of them had ever heard him defy their leader, certainly not in public.

The Gibbon turned his gaze upon Kawil. Selena knew this wasn't Miles but then who could it be? Surely Dr. Evil wasn't up to this level of disguise...?

"I will forgive your impertinence," The Gibbon said, "but my patience has limits. Why do you doubt my word?"

"Because you are not The Gibbon...I have stood by his side for many years and I know his manner and his scent. You reek of deceit. You are an enemy, hiding behind the sacred furs! You are an affront to the legacy and ideals of The Gibbon!"

What happened next occurred so fast that it took several seconds after for it to fully sink in—The Gibbon pulled a pistol from within his furs and pointed it directly at Kawil. The trigger was pulled and a projectile of death slammed right through the priest's forehead. His body flew back and struck the ground with a loud thumping sound.

Selena was the first to react, breaking the spell of stunned silence by crouching beside Kawil. He was obviously dead, his face still contorted in an expression of fury—the notion that a villain was parading about in The Gibbon's sacred garb had pushed him over the edge and caused him to take a stand that had resulted in his death.

A moment later, the warriors began shouting in disbelief. Kawil was dead...slain by The Gibbon? Could the warrior-priest's words have been true? Was this Gibbon a false one?

"Sorry about that," 'The Gibbon' said. He reached up with his free hand and began to pull at his face—it distorted and ripped before finally coming free entirely. Selena recognized the stuff as plastiderm...and the horrific visage displayed beneath it was blue-tinted and inhuman. "The dead gentleman there was right. I am not The G ibbon. You can call me Dr. Evil, instead." He pointed his gun at the group and added, "Now you may be thinking that if you all rush me at the same time, some of you will get through. That's true—but I'll kill several before then. And for what? Your precious Gibbon is dead...how else would I be wearing these skins?"

Selena wasn't listening to his words...instead, she was listening with her heart, as Kawil had urged her to do. She knew that whatever she did now could very well be the most important decision of her life and she was ready for it. From the moment her parents had been seized by those gunmen and her life had come tumbling down, everything had been building to this...another gunman, more people that she cared about depending on her, and her with the ability and the desire to do something about it.

She was up and on her feet in a blur, spinning about to knock the gun from Dr. Evil's hand. He blinked in surprise, backing away from her. He stumbled on the loose soil and lost his footing—he would have fallen then, if she hadn't seized him by The Gibbon's furs. Without a word, she yanked back, literally ripping the garments from his torso. He tumbled back, rolling down the side of the cliff and landing in a rumpled heap down in the camp. His men rushed to his side to help him up but he snarled and pushed them away.

Selena turned back to the men, holding the furs aloft. "The Gibbon is

She was spinning about to knock the gun from Dr. Evil's hand.

more than animal skins! He is a spirit that exists in every animal, every blade of grass and in the hearts of all men and women!" She slung the skins about her, cinching them tight with her belt. "I hear The Gibbon's words in my heart—and he says that we must continue to fight! He says that we must honor all those that have given their very lives so that we might live! Do you hear it, too?"

The men raised their fists and roared their approval. Their shouts grew into a frenzy when Selena threw her head back and emitted a sound that she would have never thought she was capable of releasing: it was the sound of The Gibbon, the feared cry of the jungle lord.

The Gibbon would never die.

■ ■ ■

"We have to leave. Now!" Dr. Evil snatched open the passenger side door of the truck and pulled himself inside.

"We don't have all the Prime Energy collectors onboard, sir!" one of his men said.

"Then hurry and get them loaded," Dr. Evil hissed. He heard the inhuman cry of The Gibbon and he slammed his fist into the dashboard of the truck. "Make sure the charges are ready to go—when we leave this place, we're going to dissect it down to its very atoms."

■ ■ ■

Miles cut Uliana down from her bonds, catching her when she sagged into his arms. She looked paler than usual and her eyelids looked incredibly heavy as she opened them to look up at him. "Miles…I was worried that Dr. Evil had killed you."

Brushing her hair away from her face, he said, "No, he just did his usual ranting and raving." Miles saw with some alarm that the hair he had touched fell away from her head now, landing on the floor. "What has he done to you?" he whispered.

"He drained her of those Prime Energies that he's obsessed with," Juthrbog said. The Russian's eyes were blazing with anger and Miles felt certain that if he were not still tied to the wall, he would have expressed his fury in a more physical manner. "She's going to die because you failed to stop Dr. Evil in the past, *Captain Action*." He said the codename like it was a curse and Miles couldn't really argue the point. Maybe he had made a mistake by not being more bloodthirsty…Every person that died at Evil's hands could be traced back to Miles and his morality.

"Don't...listen to him," Uliana said. She forced herself to stand on her own, though the effort looked herculean. "He's just...concerned."

"He's in love with you," Miles whispered.

Uliana merely nodded, as if the depth of her friend's feelings were well known to her. "My heart belongs...to someone else, Miles. As you know."

"You need to sit down," Miles said. "I'll cut Juthrbog loose and together we'll get you to someone that can help you..."

Uliana reached out for the wall, seeking to steady herself. "You have to stop him. If he gets away with those Prime Energies, there's no telling what he'll do...I overheard him talking about the moon mission that NASA is planning."

Another clump of hair fell away from her scalp and Miles felt his heart suddenly seize up, as if an invisible fist was squeezing it. Uliana's skin, normally so full and inviting to the touch, was becoming shriveled and leathery before his very eyes.

Uliana looked up at him and her eyes remained strong—even now, with her life ebbing away, she remained the fiery woman that had won his devotion. "Promise me, Miles...Promise me that you'll put an end to him. And...promise me that you'll try to be happy. I want you to find a woman that will treat you the way you deserve."

"Hush," he said, taking her arms in his hands. "You're not going to die. Not on my watch."

A single tear ran down the right side of her face and she smiled, even as her lips grew dry and began to split. "Promise me...."

Miles pulled her close and slid to the floor, taking her with him. She felt so light in his grip and he felt her body begin to shudder. "I promise," he said, kissing the top of her head. "I promise."

Juthrbog made a choking sound and Miles glanced up to see him staring at the two of them with a forlorn expression. The dour Russian looked heartbroken and for a moment they were joined in that emotion... but Miles could only imagine how much worse it felt for Juthrbog. Even now, at the final moment of Uliana's life, she was seeking comfort from another...he was denied even the chance to reach out to her or to say goodbye by the bonds that had been placed upon him.

"I love you, Uliana," he whispered, tearing his gaze away from Juthrbog's and focusing on the final seconds he had with Uliana. "I'm so sorry."

"You're a wonderful man," she said but her voice was so quiet that he had to strain to hear her. "That's why Dr. Evil hates you so much—because you're everything that he's not."

A strong shudder ran through her body and then it was over...he felt it immediately. Whatever made a person so much more than flesh and blood—the "soul" or "spirit" - it had departed her.

Miles held her for a moment more before setting her gently on the floor. He rose and soundlessly freed Juthrbog, who was likewise silent for a long moment. It wasn't until Captain Action started for the door that Juthrbog asked, "Where are you going?"

"To catch Dr. Evil, like she asked me to. Will you take her body back to New Lake? I think that's where she'd want to go."

Juthrbog blinked away tears and nodded. "I give you my word."

"Thank you for being there for her over these past few months," Captain Action said.

"The pleasure was all mine...Miles Drake."

Captain Action nodded. He pulled out a small device that looked like a walkie-talkie and stepped outside. Juthrbog heard him talking to someone but he wasn't concerned about the details. He had just lost the only woman that he had ever loved...and for now, that was all he could concentrate on.

Even when the sounds of renewed battle suddenly filled the air, Juthrbog didn't move, instead standing there and looking down upon Uliana's still form.

TWENTY-ONE: FLIGHT!

Selena Rubio — The Gibbon — was at the front of the descending horde. Though small in number, these jungle warriors fought with a ferocity that sent their enemies tumbling to the ground in bloody heaps. They took their cues from the woman that now embodied their sacred leader. She was a whirlwind of activity, leaping and kicking while simultaneously firing the pistol she held in her right hand. At her urging, her men seized fallen weapons and turned them against their foes...and she was grateful that Jack Oat had trained many of them in the use of firearms. Their aim was not always true but they made up for it by rapidly reloading and, when necessary, using the rifles and handguns to bludgeon the opposition.

The Gibbon spotted Captain Action emerging from one of the huts—he was using some sort of communications device and she wondered quickly who he could be calling. Surely he was out of range with such a small device to reach anyone at the Directorate. Then again, she knew that he had access to technology that was far in advance of anything the Mexican government could supply to her.

She emptied her gun's ammunition into the belly of a man that was stupid enough to block her path and then stopped at Captain Action's side. He looked at her with a haunted expression, showing no surprise that she was wearing the sacred furs. "Miles? Are you hurt?"

He turned off his radio and attached it to his belt. "She's dead. Dr. Evil used machines to drain the life right out of her."

There was no doubt about who he was talking about and Selena rubbed his shoulder. "Oh, Miles…I'm so sorry."

Captain Action gave a curt nod and drew his lightning sword. "Dr. Evil's probably gone by now but if he's not…"

A truck began to rumble through the battleground, moving so quickly that several men on both sides were nearly mowed down by the heavy vehicle. Captain Action spotted a familiar face in the passenger seat and he bolted towards the truck, leaving behind a temporarily dumbstruck Selena. The girl recovered quickly, reloading her pistol and continuing her own war against the enemy, while her friend focused on stopping his old foe from escaping.

Miles chose a path that would allow him to intersect with the one chosen by the truck's driver. The vehicle sped up at the last moment, indicating that they'd spotted him, and it roared past him but they hadn't counted on Captain Action's willingness to risk life and limb. He seized hold of the rear bumper and used it vault himself up into the covered back of the truck. The only door on the rear was of the half variety and he was able to jump past it with ease.

There was one guard in the back of the truck and he stood up with a shocked expression on his face. The man had a rifle slung over his back but he failed to grab hold of it before Captain Action was upon him, slugging him with a right hook that would have made Muhammad Ali proud. The man hit the deck and groaned. Captain Action picked up his rifle and tossed it out the rear of the truck, hoping that would dissuade the man from becoming a nuisance in the future.

The truck was filled with clear glass tubing, all of it glowing softly with

Prime Energies absorbed from the crashed meteor…and, no doubt, the Energies taken from Uliana were amongst them. For a moment, Captain Action considered smashing them with his sword but he wasn't sure what kind of effect these Energies would have—for all he knew, they might explode in a fireball that would kill everyone in the camp or worse.

Instead, he moved back to the rear of the truck and jumped up onto the half-door, using it to spring off. He scaled up onto the top of the truck and began crawling like a crab towards the cab, hurriedly sheathing his blade so he'd have both hands free. The driver must have heard his approach because he began wildly veering from side to side as they left the camp behind. Captain Action skidded across the roof before seizing hold with his fingertips. He wasn't able to avoid branches slapping against him as the truck deliberately swerved under trees with low-hanging branches.

Captain Action heard movement from behind him and he turned to see that the guard he'd slugged earlier was clambering up onto the roof of the truck. "You don't give up, do you?" he asked.

The man grinned, revealing several gaps in his teeth that indicated he had a history as a brawler. "There's a big reward for anybody that kills you, Captain Action." The fellow rose uncertainly onto his feet, pausing to make sure he had his balance before advancing on Captain Action. He kicked the roof several times, obviously trying to signal the driver to slow down—the message was received because the swerving ceased and the truck returned to the more stable dirt road.

Captain Action stood up as well, dropping into a fighting stance. The guard was easily three inches taller and a good twenty pounds heavier, all of it muscle. The man's knuckles were rough and showed signs of frequent use as mallets. "Guess there's no hope that we'll be able to talk this through?" Captain Action asked. "I mean, I did knock you on your ass just a couple of minutes ago. You don't want more of that, do you?"

The guard chuckled and spat something onto the area between Captain Action's feet. It was a bloodied tooth. "I think you owe me one of those in return, Captain. I hate to bust up that pretty smile of yours but I'm gonna do it."

Captain Action danced forward and swung a punch towards the man's nose—unfortunately, the truck's tires chose that moment to run over a dip in the road and the Captain's footing was affected. As such, his blow completely missed its target and he was left open to a retaliatory punch that hit home in his midsection, knocking all the air from his lungs.

The mercenary laughed hoarsely, obviously pleased with himself. His mood soured almost immediately because Captain Action kicked him in the shin and then drove an elbow into the side of his head. To his credit, the big man recovered quickly, blocking a follow-up punch from Captain Action.

Captain Action gasped as the man seized him by the throat, applying enough pressure that his breathing was immediately restricted. The Captain's feet were lifted off the ground and he tried to use them as weapons but in this position all they did was strike feebly at his attacker's washboard stomach.

"No jokes now, Captain?" the fellow asked. He was beaming, revealing his broken smile and bloodied gums.

The edges of Captain Action's vision were beginning to darken and he knew that he was literally moments away from passing out. He thought of Uliana…and of Selena…and of all the men and women out there that he didn't even know but who were all depending on him to stop Dr. Evil. Somehow that gave him the strength he needed to reach down and draw his lightning sword. The sunlight gleamed off the blade as he raised it high—and his opponent's eyes widened in alarm when he realized how perilous his situation really was. Captain Action brought down the weapon and it sliced right through the mercenary's arm.

The result was instant: Captain Action landed hard on the roof of the truck, suddenly able to draw in much-needed air. His enemy was staggering about, spraying blood and howling like an injured animal. Captain Action stuck out one leg and when the mercenary crossed its path, he toppled over and rolled right off the side of the truck. Captain Action looked up to see him strike the ground—still alive but in great pain. He'd need to get that wound taken care of soon or he'd bleed out.

Captain Action struggled back to his feet, turning back towards the front of the truck—what he saw nearly made him curse like a sailor.

Dr. Evil was hanging out of the passenger side seat, his door open. He was holding a pistol and taking aim at his oldest foe—and before Captain Action could react, the villain had pulled the trigger. Thankfully the bouncing road and awkward angle sent the bullet off-target. Even so, Captain Action knew that another shot would probably end his life. Gritting his teeth, he turned to the side and vaulted himself right off the truck. He landed on the hard ground in a roll and sprang up quickly but the vehicle was roaring away from him, already kicking up rocks and dirt as the driver floored the accelerator.

An unusual sound caught his attention and somewhat mollified his disappointment. It was like a jet engine, only not quite as loud—and it was very low to the ground, as if a plane was somehow skimming along on land.

Within seconds, the source of the noise came into view and despite the pain of having just lost Uliana and failing to catch Dr. Evil, Miles couldn't help but smile.

The Silver Streak lived up to its name, rocketing through the jungle until it slowed alongside Captain Action.

This was the personal vehicle of Captain Action and it was one of the most distinctive transports in the entire world. Resembling a squarish two-seater convertible, it was unusual in that it didn't have a conventional wheelbase. Rather it skimmed along the surface of the ground with antigravity technology—a Cavorite core rendered the car and its passengers virtually weightless and the vehicle then relied upon conventional jet turbines for steering and thrust. It was actually capable of true flight, though this was sometimes difficult to control—still, its operational ceiling of 20,000 feet and flight speed of 400 mph had proven useful at times. On land it could race along at 220 mph and was equally at home on water, where it could zip forward at a crisp 120 mph.

The car was blue, with a silver stripe running lengthwise down the chassis—the silver stripe was split lengthwise by a thinner red stripe, making it somewhat match the colors of Captain Action's uniform. The rear of the vehicle housed a couple of small surface to air missiles, completing the impressive package.

The Silver Streak itself was not the source of Captain Action's smile, however. It was the young man piloting the craft—Sean Walsh Barrett. Codenamed Action Boy, he was the grandson of Dr. Evil and the closest friend that Miles Drake possessed. Though only fifteen years old, he was far more skilled than many agents two and three times his age—in fact, he had recently graduated to full agent status, having wrapped up his training in record time. Due to his age, however, he was rarely given solo missions—instead, he was assigned as Captain Action's "sidekick," a role that he seemed to embrace rather than be annoyed by.

The handsome young man possessed blond hair and blue eyes. He was a lean, athletic sort, standing 5'7" and already developing the sort of muscles that women would respond to favorably. His cheerful face was partially hidden beneath his agent's beret but his physique was amply displayed in his A.C.T.I.O.N. uniform, with which somewhat resembled his mentor's garb—mostly blue, with red arms and sides, coupled with black trunks and boots.

Action Boy slid into the passenger seat so Captain Action could take his place behind the wheel. "Figured you'd want to handle the driving yourself," he said with a wink and a grin.

"Thanks." Captain Action activated the thrust and the Silver Streak shot forward like a bullet from a gun. He pushed the car to its upper limit, recklessly whipping around curves and not letting up until he spotted the truck off in the distance—from the way they were gaining on it, it seemed to have stopped near the water. The blue of the Gulf of Mexico could be clearly seen.

"You sounded pretty tense when you called me," Sean murmured. They had been in touch for the entire time that Captain Action had been in Mexico...though he knew that his mentor had kept that fact a secret from everyone, even the local agent that he'd been paired with. Shortly before he'd left into the jungle with Selena, Captain Action had asked Sean to come to Mexico with the Silver Streak and lie in wait in case he needed him. That call had finally come and Sean, who had stayed in uniform practically the whole time out of excitement, had rushed into action. "What's Dr. Evil up to this time?"

"Uliana's dead."

"Whoa." Sean swallowed and looked straight ahead. They were coming up fast on the parked truck. Now they could clearly see that the doors were wide open and the rear of the vehicle was empty—worse, it looked like whatever cargo they'd been carrying had been loaded onto a couple of speedboats which were already heading across the Gulf, towards Florida. "I'm really sorry, Miles. I...I know how you feel."

Captain Action's expression softened somewhat. Sean had nursed a massive crush for Uliana and Miles was fairly certain that she might have been the first woman that had ever caught his attention in adult fashion. Those kinds of things might seem silly or unimportant to grown-ups but Miles remembered how intense such feelings could seem to a young man.

"I know you do, pal." He reached out and gave the young man's leg a pat. "I've got a lot to tell you—but we don't have time for that now. You buckled?"

Sean sighed and pulled his shoulder belt around to lock it into place. Despite all his training, there were times when Miles still treated him like a kid—right down to making sure his seatbelt was in place. Though it was annoying at times, a part of Sean relished it...Miles was the closest thing to a father figure he had and he appreciated that the older man cared so much for him.

"Are we going to stop him this time, Miles? For good?"

Captain Action grunted as the Silver Streak rocketed right past the truck and began skimming over the surface of the Gulf. A fine spray of mist began to rise up all around them as the antigravity jets pushed downward against the water. He didn't need to ask Sean what he meant—both of them had lost loved ones to his grandfather's madness. Sean wanted to know if lethal force would be used against Dr. Evil. "I'll let you know when we reach that point, Sean."

The surprise on Action Boy's face was obvious. His mentor had always been adamant that Dr. Evil needed to be brought to justice and turned over to the authorities. "We're agents of law, Sean—whenever possible, we try to avoid being judge, jury, and executioner," was something that he'd told him more than once. For him to openly admit that that he was considering something besides that…

I'd run fast if I were you, Dr. Evil, Sean thought to himself.

TWENTY-TWO: THE CHASE

Dr. Evil twisted around in his seat. The Silver Streak was in pursuit and he knew that the vessel was faster and more maneuverable than his own. His driver was an expert but that probably wouldn't be enough to save them. "Radio the other boat and tell them to keep heading north to the extraction point."

"What about us?" the man asked, reaching for the radio. He was in his early sixties but with that kind of weather-beaten look that made it difficult for strangers to recognize his age. He could have been anywhere between 35 and 70. Nicknamed Curly because of his clean-shaven head, he was one of the few lackeys that had been in Evil's employ for multiple campaigns. Most of the villain's henchmen ended up dead for some reason.

"Slow down a bit, Curly. Let them get closer…and then I'll give them a little surprise that should rid us of them forever."

■ ■ ■

"We're in pursuit of Dr. Evil now," Action Boy said, holding the Silver Streak's radio close to his lips.

Major General Harlan James Weston replied, "We can mobilize the navy and get them there—"

"It's under control," Captain Action said, raising his voice so he'd be heard.

"Did you get that, sir?" Action Boy asked the general.

"Yes...I heard him. He didn't sound good, Sean. Has something happened that I need to know about?"

Sean glanced over at Captain Action, noting the way his mentor's jaw was clenched. "I'm sure it'll be in our report. I think it's best if you let us handle it for now."

"Very well. I trust you two to take care of this. Don't let me down."

"I'll take full responsibility for this," Captain Action called out. "I appreciate it, Harl."

There was a harrumph from the other end of the line and then it went silent—Sean knew the Major General was probably concerned and with good reason but Captain Action's use of his name had probably impressed upon him how personal this was.

Captain Action saw the two motorboats beginning to separate. The one containing the majority of the Prime Energies containers kept to its course but Dr. Evil's boat began to slow and veer off to the left. "What's he up to, I wonder?" he asked aloud.

"Probably not anything good," Sean replied, putting away the radio. "You think we could hit him with our missiles from here?"

"Possibly but I'd rather not risk it—besides if we blow his boat to smithereens, that's no guarantee that he's been dealt with. I've seen him 'die' multiple times before, remember?"

Sean blinked, straining his eyes to make out what was happening around the spray of water. "Looks like he's putting together some kind of gizmo."

Captain Action had seen it, too—and it was becoming clearer as they gained on their adversary. Dr. Evil was attaching some sort of barrel to a large upright pole that he'd fastened to the back of the motorboat. That it was a gun of some kind was pretty easy to guess—but how powerful and accurate it was, that was yet to be seen.

"Sean, I need you to take some shots at him while I try to bring us up alongside his boat. Don't let him fire that thing if you can."

Action Boy grinned and yanked out his pistol. If he felt any guilt over shooting at his grandfather, he certainly didn't let it show—though given how the man had killed Sean's parents and then tortured the boy, it was safe to assume that any familial love he might have once possessed for Tracy was long gone, Miles believed.

Action Boy fired two quick shots, both of them striking harmlessly at the side of the boat. Dr. Evil flinched visibly and turned his device towards the Silver Streak. A bolt of fiery green energy struck the water just beside the boat and caused the water to immediately turn to steam.

Realizing just how dangerous that weapon was spurred Captain Action to take a desperate maneuver. Spinning the wheel sharply to avoid another burst from Dr. Evil's gun, he brought the Silver Streak close to Evil's boat and waited until Sean had fired again—this time his projectile just barely skimmed past Evil's shoulder.

"Sean, take the wheel. We're swapping places."

To his credit, Action Boy didn't question his mentor—they timed it so that Miles leapt over him while Sean slid into Captain Action's place behind the wheel. Captain Action drew his lightning sword and held it at the ready. "Slow down and turn perpendicular to their boat—make sure I'm facing them."

"Evil will hit us for sure…"

"That's what I'm counting on, Sean. Don't try to avoid it."

Action Boy did as he was told and Dr. Evil's face seemed to light up as he realized that he had a nearly perfect opportunity to erase Captain Action from the face of the planet. He took aim and pulled the trigger.

Green energy shot forth on a direct course for Captain Action's miraculous car. At the last moment, Miles stood up in his seat and held the sword in front of him—one of its unusual properties was its ability to absorb and redirect energy…and it served its purpose perfectly this time. The lightning sword glowed brightly as the energy was drawn to it and stored within its orichalcun blade.

The two vehicles were now so close that Captain Action could have probably thrown his sword at Dr. Evil…but that wasn't the sort of attack that he had in mind. Instead, he pointed the point of his blade at his arch-foe and allowed the stored energy to shoot forth. It slammed into the villain's weapon and caused it to explode. The entire motorboat followed suit a moment later as the resulting fire caused the fuel to ignite. He hadn't intended for such an incendiary reaction but in a very real way, it was Dr. Evil's own weapon that had resulted in this outcome.

Bits of wood and metal became shrapnel, hurling in all directions. One large chunk of the boat slammed right into Captain Action's left temple, knocking him back against Sean and causing him to momentarily lose control of the Silver Streak.

Darkness crowded in around the edges of Captain Action's consciousness and he realized he was about to pass out…but at least he felt confident that Dr. Evil was dead, once and for all.

■ ■ ■

It was several hours later that the man once known as Stefan Tracy opened his eyes. The moon hung full and bloated in the sky above and water lapped at his feet. He sat up, seeing Curly's corpse, badly burned, lying nearby. All around them were pieces of their boat, along with scattered items that had been used to store the Prime Energies they'd absorbed in the jungle.

He rose unsteadily to his feet and felt around in his sodden pockets. He found a radio and hoped that it still functioned—it did and within moments he'd made contact with his men. They would come for him and his dark mission would continue…but where was Captain Action and the annoying youth that was now Action Boy? Had they been killed in the explosion? Or had they, too, washed ashore?

No matter…the other boat had contained the bulk of the stolen energy and that would be more than enough to complete his goals.

Dr. Evil began to laugh, the notes of his mirth becoming more strident and maniacal as they took hold. Soon…soon…he would be triumphant. And alive or dead, Captain Action would never be able to stop him.

TWENTY-THREE: ONE SMALL STEP

July 16, 1969

The crowds had been waiting for hours, a palpable sense of excitement in the air. Of course, the men and women at the Kennedy Space Center in Merritt Island, Florida shared that emotion but they managed to cloak their feelings behind a façade of efficiency. This was the fifth manned mission in the Apollo program but it would be the first whose purpose was to put astronauts on the surface of the moon. It was the culmination of President Kennedy's promise to do so before the end of the decade—and the press couldn't stop pointing out what a shame it was that he hadn't lived to see this day. Back in 1961, two years before his life was ended in an assassination, he had set a lofty goal, "before this decade is out, of landing a man on the Moon and returning him safely to Earth."

Liftoff was scheduled for around 9:30 a.m. Eastern Standard Time and with the weather so clear, there seemed to be little chance that they wouldn't deliver on that promise. A Saturn V rocket would take off from Launching Pad 39A, part of Launch Complex 39 site—this would propel Apollo 11 into the upper atmosphere and begin the planned 8-day roundtrip mission. The Apollo spacecraft had three parts: a command module with a cabin for the three astronauts; a service module which supported the command module with propulsion, electrical power, oxygen and water; and a lunar module that had two stages—a lower stage for landing on the moon and an upper stage to place the astronauts back into lunar orbit.

The names of the three men going on the mission were already well known around the world: Commander Neil Armstrong, Lunar Module Pilot Edwin "Buzz" Aldrin, Jr. and Command Module Pilot Michael Collins. For Collins, it was almost a matter of redemption—originally slated to be the pilot on Apollo 8, he had missed out on the mission due to a back surgery. When he was medically cleared, he was assigned to take James Lovell's position on Apollo 11.

A Saturn V rocket would take off from Launching Pad 39A...

The press had made the three men into national heroes but behind all the worship, there was the same kind of awful anticipation that sometimes drew men and women to professional racing. It wasn't simply to be there to see the triumph…they also wondered if they would witness the tragedy. What if these three brave men never made it home? The astronauts knew this, of course, but it was their trust in the engineers and mission controllers that allowed them to move forward and believe that this wouldn't be a one-way trip.

■ ■ ■

Buzz Aldrin stood before a mirror in one of NASA's locker-rooms, checking his uniform and equipment one more time. His face betrayed no worry though he did seem to be somewhat overly concerned with his appearance. He leaned close to the mirror and moved a gloved hand over his features, as if checking to make sure that he hadn't missed any spot while shaving.

"Getting ready for your close-up, Buzz?"

Aldrin looked over at Michael Collins, who was grinning. "Hey, our faces are going to be plastered all over every newspaper in the world. Nothing wrong with making sure I'll be looking my best."

Collins chuckled and then grew a bit more serious. "Just spotted Neil doing the same thing. Guess it's more important for you guys—I'm not even stepping on the moon. I'm just your cabbie while you guys get all the glory."

"You really feel that way?"

Collins broke out into another smile. "Not really. If there are any aliens out there with ray guns, you guys will take the hit and not me."

Neil Armstrong stepped into the room at that point, looking serious. "The boys upstairs say it's time to get a move on," he said, running a hand through his short-trimmed hair. All of them had gotten haircuts the day before—even Buzz, who lived up to his nickname when it came to the way he kept his hair.

Buzz turned his attention to packing up the last of his personal items that he was allowed to bring on onboard. Collins noticed him picking through them, as if he couldn't remember what he had packed. He had mentioned earlier that he planned to take communion on the moon—his pastor had given him a piece of communion bread, a sip of wine and a tiny silver chalice to aid him in the ceremony. Originally, Buzz had hoped that the communion might be shared with all those watching and listening—but the NASA head honchos had nixed that idea. NASA was currently paying a lot to fight a lawsuit brought by atheist activist Madalyn Murray O'Hair, who was angered by the public reading of Genesis by the crew of Apollo 8. Her argument was that each of the astronauts was a government employee and thus the separation of church and state should have applied.

Buzz held up the chalice and looked amused. Collins assumed there was some private joke that he was remembering. He looked over at Neil, who was also watching Buzz. For a moment the two men locked eyes and Neil gave him a smile.

"Did you notice all the extra security?" Collins asked. "There are bigwigs I've never even seen before crawling around the place."

Neil nodded. "We're a big deal, boys. I heard last night that they're afraid that the Russians might try to sabotage the mission."

Buzz gave a shrug. "I wouldn't worry about that—they've got this place locked down so tight that anybody who even looks the slightest bit Red is being detained."

Neil grunted. "Too bad they look just like us."

"Speak for yourself," Buzz replied with a grin. "I'm All-American."

Laughing, the three men gathered into a small circle and looked at one another. As mission commander, Neil was expected to set the tone for the day. "Okay, boys, I don't have to remind you about how big this is. To quote a great man, we're boldly going where no man has gone before."

Collins smirked. "Where's Yeoman Rand?"

"She's waiting onboard," Buzz said with a wink.

Neil waited until Collins had recovered from Buzz's joke. "Seriously, though, let's remember all of our training. The NASA engineers have done their part and you know that mission command's going to be giving their best. We don't need to squander it all by screwing up something simple on our end."

Buzz and Collins both nodded. The three knew their jobs—they were the best of the best. After today, they all knew that the world would never be the same.

■ ■ ■

The three men were nearly blinded by all the camera flashbulbs that went off as they began their journey to the Saturn V rocket. They waved and kept moving, the weight of the moment settling like an anvil upon their shoulders.

When they arrived at the gantry and they were out of sight of the press, Neil said, "Collins, you go on in. I want to chat with Buzz for a moment."

Collins stopped in surprise but he gave a nod and boarded. He assumed that they were going to go over the procedure for what would happen when they landed—behind the scenes, there had been some jockeying back and forth about which man would be the first to set foot on the moon. It was all a moot concern for Collins since the plan was for him to stay on board for the entire flight but he knew that both Neil and Buzz wanted to go down in the history books and he couldn't really blame them.

"What's the problem, Neil?" Buzz asked. "If kinda late in the game to start getting cold feet."

"I know you replaced Collins' carry-on items with those canisters of Prime Energy...what I don't know is what your plan ultimately is. At first I assumed you wanted to prevent the rocket from launching...but you're actually planning to go to the moon. Why?"

Buzz stared hard at Neil and then he shook his head in obvious amazement. "I should have known you'd survived—if I did, why shouldn't you? I give you credit, though, Captain Action...I didn't expect you to take Armstrong's place."

"He's in on it—if all goes the way it's supposed to, the mission will go off without a hitch. I'll swap out with him before the launch. Speaking of which, Aldrin is fine, too. We found him drugged and unconscious about an hour ago."

Dr. Evil, still wearing the face of the astronaut, spread his arms out wide. "You have caught me. Congratulations. I suppose now is when I share my brilliant plan with you?"

"Unless you'd rather I knocked you out and then you talked from behind bars in prison."

Both men were circling each other, using the pretense of talking as an excuse to look for an opening. The hate between them was almost palpable. Despite all of their successes, each considered the other to be responsible for many of their failures. "My unique physiology allows me to survive in environments that would be fatal to normal humans—including the void of deep space. I don't need to eat or breathe. I plan to use that to my advantage. Using the Prime Energies I secured from the Yucatan, I'm going to transform the moon into my new base of operations—eventually, I'll give it an atmosphere suitable for my minions to survive in. Until then, I'll live there alone...sending down death from above whenever mankind refuses my demands!"

Even if Captain Action hadn't already known that his old enemy lurked behind Buzz's face, the familiar glint of madness in his eyes would have been proof enough of his identity.

"You're insane."

"The truly brilliant are always called that by the rabble."

"Is that what I am? The rabble?"

Dr. Evil paused before answering. "No. You're not, Captain Action. You're more than that—I have to grant you that distinction. You're my greatest enemy and it's fitting that I have to kill you before I can have my ultimate triumph."

Without any further preamble, Dr. Evil lunged for Captain Action.

TWENTY-FOUR: THE FINAL COUNTDOWN

Captain Action dodged to the left avoiding a right hand from Dr. Evil that would have knocked him right on his posterior. Realizing that Evil was momentarily off-balance, the Captain drove his elbow hard against the villain's skull. As Evil grunted in pain, Captain Action seized the man's face and scratched with his nails, digging deep gouges in the plastiderm. Evil's blue skin was revealed as a large flap of pseudo-flesh was ripped away.

Dr. Evil reached into his astronaut's uniform and withdrew a small knife with a serrated edge. With a nasty snarl, he stabbed right at Captain Action's heart. He missed his mark when the hero jerked back but he still managed to draw blood, slicing right through the thick padding of "Neil's" uniform.

■ ■ ■

At that moment Collins decided to stick his head out of the rocket. "What's taking you guys so long?" he asked. What he saw made his eyes widen in disbelief: there was Neil and Buzz, obviously in a furious fight to the death. Even stranger, part of Buzz's face had been ripped away… but rather than blood and sinew being revealed, there was a second set of features beneath.

…And they were *blue*!

"Get back into the vehicle!" Armstrong shouted, though his voice sounded *different*.

Collins hesitated, torn between a desire for self-preservation and his innate heroism. In the end, he heard an unfamiliar voice come over the loudspeaker: "Commander Collins, please return to your position on the ship."

With a frown, Collins complied, yanking the door shut behind him. For the past six months, he'd carried a terrifying fear within his heart, afraid to give voice to it: what if Buzz and Neil weren't able to make it back after their moonwalk? Collins had already decided that he wouldn't commit suicide out there in space…he'd return to earth, even if it meant he'd a marked man for the rest of his life. People would find a way to blame him for the failure of the mission but he knew that the point of this, of showing mankind that humanity could break free of the earth's bonds and explore the greater universe were worth the risk. He thought that Neil and Buzz shared that conviction…but what the hell was happening out there?

He returned to his seat and buckled up, not knowing what else to do. Was all their hard work over the past few months about to go up in smoke?

■ ■ ■

Captain Action heard Weston's voice over the loudspeaker and he was gratified to know that his boss was monitoring the situation. No doubt security personnel, including Action Boy, were waiting in the wings to swoop in and try to stop the flight if he were to fall in battle with Dr. Evil. Sadly, he wasn't sure they'd be able to stop the villain—he had probably installed safeguards against the mission being scuttled.

He dropped into a fighting stance and began circling to his right. Evil moved forward, throwing out a right fist in a feint and then whipping a roundhouse kick to Captain Action's left thigh. He staggered slightly and Evil threw a quick backhand that smashed against his left temple. His vision swam and his knees buckled but he managed to bounce away, putting a small bit of distance between him and Dr. Evil.

The move didn't provide much relief, however, as Dr. Evil struck out with his knife, hurling it with deadly accuracy. It stung his right forearm and remained lodged there until Captain Action yanked it out and tossed it aside. He instantly regretted dispensing with the weapon because he saw that Dr. Evil had pulled out yet another weapon—this one a small baton, similar to the nightsticks used by inner city police officers.

Dr. Evil chuckled and brandished the baton in his right hand. "I've been taking fighting lessons, Captain—can you tell?"

"Not really," he taunted. "You still move as gracefully as a bull in a china shop."

Evil roared and moved forward, raising the baton over his head.

Captain Action was ready and delivered a double left jab into the man's throat. The blows managed to stun him and Captain Action followed up with a right cross that rattled his knuckles and caused Evil to take several steps back.

Evil reached up to rub the back of his hand across his lips, tearing away more of the plastiderm and smearing blood across his cheek. "Did your girlfriend die, Captain? I bet she did…she whimpered so much as I drained the energy from her. You should have seen the look on her face. I think she kind of enjoyed it, though. The pain, I mean. I think she was one of *those* girls."

Despite his training, Captain Action saw red when he heard his enemy's inflammatory ranting—he danced forward, firing off another jab but Evil blocked it with ease and smacked an open palm into Captain Action's face. Evil then pivoted and threw another kick, this time striking the Captain in the midsection.

Captain Action backpedaled, trying to catch his breath. It hurt every time he inhaled and he knew that he had at least a couple of broken ribs. He knew he had to fight through the pain, though—losing here was simply not an option.

Evil rushed forward but Captain Action met his approach with a snapping front kick to his chest. The impact of the blow caused Evil to veer sideways and Captain Action stepped in to deliver quick one-two punch combination. He followed up with a left hook that smashed into the madman's nostrils.

Dr. Evil looked unsteady for a moment, blood beginning to drip in dark blue raindrops from his nose.

The two opponents circled each cautiously and Captain Action sensed that Evil was beginning to tire—no matter how much training he'd received, the man once known as Stefan Tracy could never hope to match Captain Action's years of battle experience.

The villain feinted again with a backhand, then followed with another spinning kick. This time, Captain Action leaned back and Evil's foot sailed over his shoulder and head. When Evil touched the platform again, Captain Action stepped inside and delivered a three-punch combination to the gut before sending a right cross to his enemy's jaw as he backed away.

Evil looked at Captain Action with wariness now as they circled each other once again. With startling speed, the mad scientist leaped forward, his right leg striking his arch-foe hard in the chest. The stunning force of the blow sent Captain Action flying backward so he rolled with the movement, doing a backward somersault that left him standing on his feet.

Captain Action felt a twinge in his back and realized that he, too, was beginning to slow down. The exertion coupled with being stabbed and having his ribs cracked was making this fight a closer one than he'd anticipated.

Dr. Evil was slowly moving towards his foe. "It's strange to think that this will be our final battle, isn't it? For so long we've seen each other's faces in our dreams...plotted what we would say to one another when we next came to blows. And now it's coming to the end."

Captain Action felt his back come up against one of the gantry's metal beams. There was no place to go—one way or another, Evil was right: this would be the end of it. "It's not too late, Tracy. We can get you help... whatever really happened to you it unsettled your mind. The Directorate has the best shrinks that money can buy. I give you my word that nobody would rest until you were cured."

"Cured?" Evil replied with a laugh. "My dear boy, you and the rest of humanity are the diseased ones. I'm the cure for what you have—I'm the hammer that will drive all of you into your proper positions."

"And what position is that?"

"Serving your betters."

Dr. Evil whirled the baton about in a fast figure-eight motion. The move ended with one end tucked beneath his right armpit, his left hand extended forward. With a cocky grin, he gestured for Captain Action to come to him. The move was obviously intended to be an impressive one but Captain Action couldn't stop grinning—Dr. Evil had obviously tired of being physically bested by Miles and had taken great pains to try and make himself his equal. He still came across as someone whose main inspiration for his fighting style had come from bad cinema.

Captain Action looked about desperately for anything that could counter the staff but all he saw was the knife, which was too far away to be of use. His foot scraped against something and he looked down to see a small steel wrench. It most likely had fallen from one of the maintenance crew's tool belt. He seized upon it, realizing that the wrench might buy him some time. He scooped it up and threw it with all his might, striking Dr. Evil in his left eye. The villain released a cry of surprise and pain, his free hand coming up immediately to clutch at his face.

Rather than slowing him down, the attack seemed to spur Dr. Evil to greater action. Evil surged towards him with obvious anger, the baton whirling about in front of him. Captain action tried to dodge the blows but the staff collided with his leg, then his abdomen and finally the corner of his chin. The Captain tried to roll with the attack and he hit the platform with a grunt, rolling to his right just in time to avoid a crushing thrust as the end of the baton slammed into the floor next to his head. He stretched out with his feet, wrapping them around the closest of his opponent's legs. He used a scissor-like move to send the mad scientist sprawling, the baton slipping from his grip. Captain Action seized hold of it as Evil made it back to his feet and also grabbed hold of the weapon, his hands opposite Captain Action's.

The two opponents pulled, fighting for control of the weapon, and Captain Action felt a sharp pain in his side. This back-and-forth tugging was doing awful things to his shattered ribcage and he knew that he wouldn't be able to stand the pain much longer.

Miles hated to resort to fighting dirty but victory was more important than abiding by any kind of personal ethics at this point. He drew up his knee and drove it hard into his enemy's crotch. The effect was immediate, as a look of agony passed over Evil's face, making his eyes bulge. He managed to sneak his foot into the villain's gut and twisted back, using Evil's grip on the baton to help propel him over Captain Action in a judo throw.

Evil landed in a heap on the gantry and Captain Action sprang to his feet, gripping the baton like he was Hammering Hank Aaron. When Evil rose to meet him, the Captain swung for the fences, putting everything he had in the blow. The baton caught Dr. Evil on his left temple and he staggered back, landing with a thud.

Captain Action stood over his fallen foe, baton still in hand. This was the moment of choice…one solid blow to the unconscious man's skull and it would all be over. The world would never again be menaced by Stefan Tracy's madness.

Or he could truss him up and turn him over to A.C.T.I.O.N. As he'd told Dr. Evil, the boys at the Directorate might be able to find a way to restore him to something resembling his old self. Of course, that would lead to the possibility that Evil might fake his reformation or, even worse, find a way to escape his prison.

There had to be a way to rid the world of the danger without making Captain Action into a murderer…because that's what this would be if he were to strike now. Killing in the heat of battle was one thing but to do it when Evil were helpless? Even if done for all the right reasons, that would be tantamount to murder, pure and simple.

Captain Action suddenly grinned and looked at the Saturn V. An idea was forming in his mind…a way that would both protect the world and also keep Miles from becoming a murderer.

■ ■ ■

At 9:32 a.m., the massive Saturn V rocket blasted off on its history-making mission. Onboard were three of the bravest men who ever lived: Michael Collins, Buzz Aldrin and Neil Armstrong. The latter two had been checked out by medical staff and loaded onto the vessel via a route that wasn't seen by the public. Collins would get his explanation, though it was highly classified and no one on the outside would ever know how close the mission came to being compromised.

History would record the event as one of the seminal moments in human ingenuity and bravery. The three crewmembers would be treated like royalty upon their return and with good reason…but history would not tell the full tale of what happened on the moon.

There was someone else onboard Apollo 11.

Dr. Stefan Tracy, securely bound, was going to be taken to the moon just as he'd planned…but he would be left behind when the crew returned to earth. His unique physiology would allow him to exist without food or air but he'd be alone for the rest of eternity. This enforced form of solitary confinement might be considered the ultimate cruelty, but Captain Action felt confident that the punishment fit his many crimes. Perhaps even more.

The war between the enemies had finally come to an end…and the victor was all of humanity.

TWENTY-FIVE: CODA

It seemed somehow fitting that a heavy rain was falling when Miles Drake drove the Silver Streak into the jungles of the Yucatan. Sean was at his side, keeping his thoughts to himself. Miles appreciated that—there were times when a man didn't want to share his inner turmoil. He needed to stew in it for a while before it felt right to talk about such things aloud. Sean understood and respected that—he didn't push his mentor.

In the aftermath of Dr. Evil's defeat, the Apollo 11 mission had gone off without a hitch. Already Neil Armstrong's words upon touching the lunar surface had acquired a sort of almost holy importance: "That's one small step for man, one giant leap for mankind." Miles knew that Neil was mighty chagrined to have made a tiny mistake in his wording—he had left out the important letter 'a' in the phrase 'that's one small step for *a* man," and now the sentence didn't really make much sense since man and mankind would be interchangeable the way he said it. Upon being informed of his mistake, he had at first insisted that he'd said the 'a' but after listening to the recording, he'd conceded his error. Still, no one else seemed to care.

The Silver Streak pulled into what remained of The Gibbon's village. Repairs were currently underway and the survivors seemed to be in good spirits when they recognized Captain Action. Men, women and children crowded around the unusual vehicle as it came to a stop and despite the rain that pelted them, Miles and Sean both broke into grins.

After a few moments of saying hello—and allowing Miles the opportunity to check on the young friend he'd made, whose mother had been injured—he and Sean entered The Gibbon's cave. There they found Selena, though she wore the ceremonial skins and mask of the jungle lord. She had been sitting on the throne, looking through a set of ancient writings, but upon seeing her friend, she rose and embraced Miles. It was a long hug and Sean smirked for a moment—his mentor had a way of impressing women and he could only hope to do half as well with the fairer sex.

"You're soaking wet," Selena said as she pulled away.

"It's raining, in case you hadn't noticed," Miles replied. "You look good."

Selena held out her arms and did a little spin. "You think so? It's not really my usual style but I like to think I make it work."

"Is this really what you plan on doing? Staying out here and pretending to be The Gibbon?"

Selena crossed her arms over her chest. "I'm not 'pretending' to be anything, Miles. And, yes, I do plan to stay out here. It's strange but Kawil was right—wearing this, seeing the loyalty that it inspires, it changes you. I want to help them protect their homes. I don't know how much longer it can last but I'm going to do my best. The world is changing so fast and there's so little in the way of justice out here in the wild…The Gibbon is still needed."

"If you're happy, then I'm happy for you," Miles said earnestly. Sean cleared his throat and the adults turned to face him. "This is Sean," Miles said. "He's the young juvenile delinquent I told you about."

Sean's eyes opened wide in shock, which elicited a laugh from Selena. "He's teasing you," she said. She offered a hand and he shook it, obviously infatuated by her beauty…and the fact that The Gibbon outfit clung to her curves in a highly suggestive manner. "I've heard only good things about Action Boy."

"It's been the same about you," he said.

"Oh," she exclaimed, "he's a charmer, just like you, Miles."

A couple of men entered the cave, carrying wooden chairs. They set them up near the throne and everyone took a seat after the men had left.

"Did you go to New Lake?" Selena asked quietly, gauging the captain's reaction.

Miles shook his head. "No. I thought about it but I didn't want to intrude. I'm sure that Uliana's people have their ceremonies for the dead but they're not mine. Sean and I went out to the mining camp this morning and I said goodbye to her there. I did get a message from Juthrbog, though. It was pretty stilted but I think in his own way, he was apologizing for the things he said to me."

Sean looked about the cave and asked, "You worked for the Mexican government, right?"

"Si."

"Are they okay with their top agent quitting to go live in the jungle?"

"They were *cabreado*," she laughed.

"What does that mean?" the young man asked.

Miles held up a hand. "Let's just say they were less than enthused and leave it at that." He looked at Selena and smiled. "You're a bad influence, Selena."

"I have to admit that he wouldn't be the first young man that I've led astray." She grew serious and asked, "Do you want to stay, Miles? With me?"

Miles blushed furiously. "Aren't I a little old for you? I seem to recall you making that implication a few dozen times."

"You wouldn't have to be my lover," she replied with an impish smile. "Though I'm sure someone of your advanced age might be able to teach me a thing or two…but you'd be able to stay under your own terms. Kawil is dead and The Gibbon needs an advisor. Besides, you've defeated Dr. Evil at last. It's time you took time for you. Deal with your losses and decide what you want to do with your life."

Miles glanced at Sean and realized the young man was watching him closely, wondering how his mentor might react. Selena was gorgeous and the offer was certainly an enticing one—and not just because of the possibility of getting closer to the young woman. Miles had, in fact, felt a bit of a disconnect from the Directorate since his victory over Dr. Evil. The villain was trapped on the lunar surface and would never harm anyone ever again…maybe it was time for Captain Action to be put out to pasture.

He tried to picture himself out of uniform, living here in the jungles. It might be acceptable for a brief period but he knew that he'd begin to chafe before long. He wasn't meant for rest…his soul yearned for adventure. He reached out and took Selena's hand in his. "I appreciate the offer, Selena. In fact, I might surprise you by visiting you from time to time. I'm not ready to step away from A.C.T.I.O.N., though. Sean might graduate from Action Boy to Captain Action someday but not quite yet—he's still a little wet behind the ears. Isn't that right, Sean?"

Action Boy grinned, taking the ribbing good-naturedly. "Uh, sure, Miles. I probably need a few more months of training before taking over for you."

Selena nodded as if she had already known what the answer would be. She stood up and strode towards the mouth of the cave. The men looked at each other quickly and then hurried after her. She stepped outside and the rain ceased almost immediately—in fact, it was eerie the way the skies seemed to react to her presence. For a brief second, Miles wondered if there might be something to those old legends—for Selena somehow seemed taller and more powerful in those furs.

She looked over her shoulder at Miles for a moment before facing the men and women of her new home. Then she threw her head back and unleashed an inhuman call, the cry of The Gibbon…

And throughout the jungle, the animals seemed to answer her. The air was filled with a cacophony of sound as she called out to them—birds, jaguars, monkeys and more all channeled their voices into the sky.

The jungle was under the protection of The Gibbon and heaven help those that sought to commit evil under her gaze.

THE END

NEW BLOOD

The story of Captain Action has always been about new blood.
Take a look back and you'll see what I mean: After Captain Action's introduction as a 12" action figure to give GI Joe a rough time on the toy shelf battlefield in 1966, he was popular enough with kids to warrant some new blood in his line in 1967, namely Action Boy, the Silver Streak, and the Super Queen female figures. Though ultimately the additions didn't keep the good captain alive past 1968, that blood infusion added to his collectible nature many years later.

After that, new blood would become something of a revolving door for CA.

Over many returns and many owners, the captain would receive numerous transfusions of fresh corpuscles in the form of new toys and new stories, leading right up to one of the healthiest times for him since his inception, namely the 2005 acquisition of the property by "retropeneurs" Ed Catto and Joe Ahearn. They not only revived the toy line, but also added in new comic book tales and other collectibles. Life was suddenly good again for Captain Action, all because of, yes, some new blood.

Flash forward a bit to my own small wrinkle in that history of blood transfusions.

On January 24th of 2012, I sent an email to Joe and Ed that read in part:

"My idea is a good, old-fashioned pulp tale with CA, set either in the 60s or even farther back, in the 30s or 40s…I imagine the story to be straightforward pulp, more of a Doc Savage-type adventure than a Shadow mystery, but that said, I think CA lends himself to just about anything."

To which Ed replied: "That could be really fun, Jim."

And then we were off to the races with an infusion of new blood and soon Captain Action was starring in his very first pulp adventure prose novel, RIDDLE OF THE GLOWING MEN, and later, HEARTS OF THE RISING SUN.

Now, let's move this right up to now, the present day.

What you're holding in your hot little hands is the latest batch of plasma to run through the captain's fictional veins. No, not just that it's the third CA novel, but more specifically that extra name on the cover: Barry Reese.

Barry's not only some new blood for the saga, in my opinion he's a whole blood bank in himself.

When I found myself unable to attack the third CA novel for various and sundry reasons, I asked Barry to jump onboard this crazy train and take the throttle while I pumped some coal into the boiler. He jumped at my invitation and we've never looked back once. I had an outline for the novel and knew where I wanted it to go, and Barry, in his infinite wisdom saw what I was suggesting and ran with it.

Boy, did he run with it. I'm here to tell you that while the basic course of the story is mine, its Barry who infused it with atmosphere, action, and foremost of all, character. I wanted a new female lead in the book, and Barry created La Marposa. I wanted a cool jungle lord in the story, and Barry created the Gibbon. I wanted a spy-who-never-came-in-from-the-cold in the middle of it, and Barry created Jack Oat.

I can't stress this enough: the rough design of these folks was me, but these incredible character personalities and their histories are all Barry. I provided oversight to insure that Cap and Doc Evil and Sean and Uliana all talked and acted like the same people we met and adventured with in the first two novels, but beyond that, Mr. Reese brought all of his incredible pulp experience as a novelist in his own right (or is that "write"?) to flesh out everyone else you meet here in this book for the first time.

And, hopefully, it won't be the last time. If I have my druthers, I'll be reading more adventures with La Marposa and the Gibbon before too long. And Captain Action, of course.

That, none-too-gentle readers, is up to you. If CA's to receive yet more new blood, you have to make your voices heard.

Let's not have any bad blood between us, as I bow out gracefully and bid farewell to my dear, dear pal Miles Drake—let's only have new blood.

My most sincere thanks for years of action to Ed Catto, Joe Ahearn, Ron Fortier, Rob Davis, Becky Beard, Nick Runge, Michael Youngblood, and my good, good pulp pal and my savior, Barry Reese.

Into Action!

Jim Beard – May 2017

ABOUT OUR CREATORS

AUTHORS –

BARRY REESE - is an award-winning author whose work has spanned genres such as horror, science fiction and westerns. He is best known for his shared universe of pulp adventure novels, which includes the adventures of Lazarus Gray, The Peregrine and Gravedigger. He can be found online at barryreese.net

JIM BEARD - A native Toledoan, Jim Beard was introduced to comic books at an early age by his father, who passed on to him a love for the medium and the pulp characters who preceded it. After decades of reading, collecting and dissecting comics, Jim became a published writer when he sold a story to DC Comics in 2002. Since that time he's written official *Star Wars* and *Ghostbusters* comic stories and contributed articles and essays to several volumes of comic book history.

His work includes GOTHAM CITY 14 MILES, a book of essays on the 1966 Batman TV series, SGT. JANUS, SPIRIT-BREAKER, a collection of pulp ghost stories featuring his own Edwardian occult detective, CAPTAIN ACTION: RIDDLE OF THE GLOWING MEN, the first pulp prose novel based on the classic 1960s action figure; and MONSTER EARTH, a shared-world anthology of giant monster tales.

Currently, Jim provides regular content for Marvel.com, the official Marvel Comics website, is a regular columnist for Toledo Free Press and has founded Flinch Press, publisher of "in-your-face pulp-style adventure fiction," with partner John Bruening. Please visit him at http://sgtjanus. blogspot.com and on Facebook at http://facebook.com/thebeardjimbeard

INTERIOR ILLUSTRATIONS—

ROB DAVIS - began his professional art career doing illustrations for role-playing games in the late 1980's. Not long after he began lettering and inking, then penciling comics for a number of small black and white comics publishers—most notably for Eternity Comics, which eventually became Malibu Comics in the 1990's, on their book SCIMIDAR with writer R.A. Jones. Branching out to other black and white publishers and eventually working at both DC and Marvel Rob worked on likeness intensive comics like TV adaptations of QUANTUM LEAP and STAR TREK's many incarnations mostly on the DEEP SPACE NINE comics for Malibu. At Marvel he worked on the Saturday morning cartoon adaptation PIRATES OF DARK WATER. After the comics industry implosion in the late 1990's Rob picked up work on video games, advertising illustration and T-shirt design as well as some small press comics like ROBYN OF SHERWOOD for Caliber. Rob continues to do the odd self-published comic book as well as publisher and designer for his small-press production REDBUD STUDIO COMICS. Rob is Art Director, Designer and Illustrator for the New Pulp production outfit AIRSHIP 27 partnered with writer/editor Ron Fortier. Rob is the recipient of the PULP FACTORY AWARD for "Best Interior Illustrations" in 2010 and 2014 for his work on SHERLOCK HOLMES: CONSULTING DETECTIVE and has been nominated for the same award every year since its inception. He works and lives in central Missouri with his wife and two children.

For examples of his work surf to: robmdavis.com

COVER ARTIST –

TED HAMMOND - is a Canadian artist who has been creating amazing art for over twenty years. His work has appeared in magazines, ads, books and graphic novels just to name a few. Go to (www.tedhammond.com) to contact him and check out more of his work!

Super-spy and master of disguise, Miles Drake, aka Captain Action investigates the "Riddle of the Glowing Men," by writer Jim Beard. Foreign assassins are sent to kill Captain Action and though he manages to defeat them, it is their lifeless bodies that pose the greater mystery as they give off a green, glowing radiation.

Teamed with a beautiful and seductive Russian Agent, Captain Action travels to the barren, frozen wastelands of Siberia where the secret behind the glowing men lies buried in a fantastic, lost underground world. It is a secret also pursued by his most dangerous nemesis, the insidious Dr. Evil. What is this strange power hidden beneath the earth that could destroy all of mankind and who will unlock its mysteries first?

PULP FICTION FOR A NEW GENERATION!
AVAILABLE AT AMAZON.COM AND AS AN EBOOK PDF AT AIRSHIP27HANGAR.COM

While on assignment in Japan, Captain Action™ is haunted by the woman he loved and lost years ago in the underground kingdom beneath Siberia. When she mysteriously begins reappearing during his clandestine mission to witness a newly discovered power source, agent Miles Drake begins to question his own sanity.

Forces are at work to steal two naturally formed energy stones whose limitless power in the wrong hands could destroy the world. When he begins to suspect his alien nemesis, Dr. Evil, is behind these attacks, Drake has to utilize his most daring disguises ever to learn the truth and ally himself with an old vigilante hero from the past.

Now the one and only Captain Action must walk a delicate tightrope between old and new allies while attempting to discover the source of the threat to the Hearts of the Rising Sun. If he fails, mankind is doomed!

Situated in the rural back country of Edwardian England is an old, mysterious house whose unique owner earns his living as a Spirit-Breaker, a hunter of ghosts. A former military veteran, Sgt. Roman Janus has devoted his life to aid those haunted, both emotionally and physically by obsessive wraiths whose spirits are still anchored to our world.

At the end of the first book, SGT. JANUS – SPIRIT BREAKER, our intrepid hero mysteriously vanished into another realm never to be seen again. almost a full year later, a dark haired beauty, with no memory of her own identity, suddenly appears and begins assuming Janus' role in seeking out troublesome poltergeist and laying them to rest. Aided by a young clerk named Joshua, this mysterious Lady Janus possesses personal knowledge known only to the missing occultist. Who is this strange, daring woman? Is she Janus reincarnated? Or is she something even more sinister?